A CREEPY BOSS, RUBBERY EGGS, AND EXPLODING HEADS

A STORY OF POSSESSION

WRITTEN BY LEX TIPTON

Book Cover by

Contact: TiptonLex@Gmail.com

Website: www.LexTiptonBooks.com

First Edition 2024

First off, I would like to thank you for being intrigued enough about the title to read the preface, but I find it to be of the utmost importance to provide a detailed trigger warning before continuing onto the actual preface. This book contains graphic scenes of physical abuse, emotional abuse, substance abuse, sexual abuse, gore, murder, and other taboo subject matter. If you are not in the state of mind to read scenes containing these triggers, I'd personally advise putting this book back on the shelf and either not touching this book or approaching it another time (The latter option would be greatly appreciated, however).

Secondly, I don't want you to get the wrong idea about this book. I can imagine that a number of readers out there will perceive this book as a trauma fantasy of sorts. Some sort of demented smut or snuff work. My goals are vehemently against that. My goal with this book is to capture the experience of grieving over the loss of your own autonomy to an extreme extent. Doing everything one can to gain control back over themselves, but losing even more than what was left with them after their experience. Extreme content for extreme emotions towards extreme subject matter.

There are two sexual acts in this book that happen to be non-consensual and non-penetrative. I despise scenes depicting sexual assault, as they're often used distastefully for shock factor or are just poorly executed. However, I've deemed these scenes necessary for narrative and immersive purposes. All other references to sex as they occur are kept ambiguous and cut out, as they are not important to the narrative or the plot. I've attempted to approach this sensitive subject matter with as much respect and care as one can in a for-profit product. I wish for this book to not be used for fantasy or sexual fulfillment.

Thirdly, This book does not finish with a happy ending. A big fear of mine, something that truly shakes me to my core, is experiencing something that prohibits me from moving on. Choosing to rot and seeth in a pool of anguish, hatred, cynicism, and finding comfort in the void rather than pursuing fulfilling goals and connections. A lived experience I wish to never go back to. This book is a reflection of that fear, which is why I've decided to label this work as a "horror novela". This is not to say that one who's experienced this cannot live happily past the trauma, but our protagonist is not granted that blessing. If you or a loved one is currently in need of assistance, I push the notion that it is never too late to have your happy ending and to do what one can to help yourself and others. Nobody is expected to do everything, but everyone should do something. On the following pages are some hotlines and resources if you are in need of them. Thank you for reading this preface and I hope you find something worthwhile in my words.

Travel happy,
Lex Tipton

National Suicide Prevention Lifeline

Call: 988
Available 24/7

LGBT National Coming Out Support Hotline

888-OUT-LGBT (888-688-5428)

LGBT National Help Center

Youth Talkline: 800-246-7743
Senior Hotline: 888-234-7243
Monday thru Friday, 4pm to midnight ET; ; Saturday
from noon to 5pm ET

SAGE LGBT Elder Hotline

1-877-360-LGBT (5428)
Connects LGBT elders and caretakers with friendly
responders who are ready to listen. Available 24/7,
in English and Spanish, with translation in 180
languages.

Trans Lifeline

Trans Lifeline's Hotline is a confidential 24/7 peer
support phone service run by trans people for trans
and questioning people. Call us if you need
someone trans to talk to, even if you're not in crisis
or if you're not sure you're trans.
1-877-565-8860 (United States)
1-877-330-6366 (Canada)
Oprime 2 para hablar con unx operadxr en español.

Trevor Project

Phone: 1-866-488-7386
Text START to 678-678

<u>**AWARENESS**</u>
www.wristband.com/content/domestic-violence-awa
reness.
A website with links to many domestic violence
resources and guidelines,
As well as warning signs of abuse.

<u>**National Domestic Violence Hotline**</u>
Languages: English, Spanish and 200+ through
interpretation service
Hours: 24/7
Call 800-799-7233

<u>**National Drug Helpline**</u>
<u>**Substance Abuse and Addiction Hotline**</u>
Hours: 24/7
Call 1-844-289-0879
www.DrugHelpline.org

A Creepy Boss, Rubbery Eggs, and Exploding Heads: A Story of Possession

By Lex Tipton

Dedicated to my dear friends, Kristen and Mark.
Thank you both for helping me at my most vulnerable times and encouraging me to move forward through all these years. I truly don't know where I would be without your friendship.

I'd like to give my endless appreciation to my parents. For everything they've done and continue to do to provide love and care to all their children and their community. You're both extraordinary.

There's a moment that occurs every morning as I wake up, hidden within the form of warmth that encapsulates my body as my consciousness is pulled to the forefront. My brain flashes with all the tasks that I have to get done not only that day, but this week, this month, this life. I'm watching clips of myself crawling out of bed, brushing my teeth, feeding the dog that I wish to adopt in the future, calling my dentist, finishing paying my car loan, finding friends to share life with and how. Reminiscent of a sped-up montage sequence in a movie.

My stomach starts to shift and turn into a slight nausea, and my brows furrow until I let out a small audible groan to clear the phlegm that pooled in my throat through the night. I try my best to not wake my husband with the chaos of my awakening. My face relaxes again and my eyes catch their first breath of stimuli: The first thing I see in the veil of darkness is the dust dancing through beams of light cutting through window blinds. It's from a car passing by outside. It's not uncommon for me to wake to this sound when it rains. I can hear the car whizzing on the wet pavement. The rubber of the tires drags against cement and vibrates through the glass of the window, I feel a rattle through my bones. My brain finally catches up with my surroundings as the beams of light scans across the bedroom's walls and ceiling. My husband Lucas has his arm draped over my side from behind. He pulls me closer into his spoon and his hot breath creeps from my neck down to my shoulder. His morning breath stings my nose, but its heat makes the rest of my body feel colder in this dark room. A shiver runs through my body and my hairs stand on end as I relax into his warmth. His skin is tacky from holding me all night. Within my sense of safety and security flickers a spark of arousal in the back of my brain. A short respite from my morning anxiousness before it quickly returns. The inside of my chest begs the rest of my body to act. I need something to do.

"Lucas… Lucas, darli--" *oh fuck, phlegm.* I take a moment to clear my throat and readjust my approach to put on the best soft sultry voice I can muster this early in the morning.

"Lucas", I try exclaiming again. "Are you awake, darling? Would you like to have another go around?"

"Heerrgh… Uhmm," he mumbles and pulls his arm away. His body turns facing the ceiling as he yawns awake. "Wow, you're awake early. Did my alarm even go off?" he asks.

I'm impatient. This anxious pressure is pushing me. I need to move around and my body is burning. I drop my sultry act. "Lucas, do you want to fuck again?" I pester as I turn around onto my other arm to face him. Was that too stern? Ugh, maybe.

With his eyes closed, his brows furrowed and his lips purse for a moment of thought, however. His eyes finally open. "Ummm… Sure… Yeah, sure. Don't think I did a good enough job earlier? What time is it?"

"No", I say, "You did fine, but I want to make sure we get a positive result this time."

I glance over at his alarm clock sitting behind him on his night stand.

"It's 3:50 in the morning, Lucas."

"Well okay. As long as I did a good job, honey." He chuckles and he leans into tired puppy dog eyes.

"Oh, hush you prick!" I playfully slap my hand onto his chest to punish his tease. "Shut up and let me get on top of you."

Chapter 1

Rubbery Eggs

7:23 am

Lucas burnt the bacon. Again. In the many ways he needs to elate my life, oftentimes his attempts at breakfasts are his downfall, but it's one of those idiosyncrasies that makes home feel like home. Like a cheap white elephant gift: the weird-smelling candle you received for Christmas last year that currently serves as a bookshelf reminder of the friend that got it for you. More often than not you use it to cover the smell of cat piss in your living room despite it being that scent you hate so much. The sharp-scented stinge of carbonized bacon and heavy smell of egg feels like a small hometown return. Bittersweet. Just like this morning's (and let's be honest, most day's) coffee.

We moved into this apartment two years ago, shortly after getting married. It was our "fresh start" excuse for spending more money on a larger space.

Something he had been eager to do for a while and a compromise I was willing to see him smile over. We had been living together for three years before that, and dating for a year before that, totaling six years of some of the happiest hunky-dorey married years of my life. The latest chapter is the most nerve-wracking. We'll have a child to call our own, hopefully.

The apartment has two bedrooms, one and a half bathrooms, a roomy high-ceiling living room attached to the kitchen with a kitchen island separating the two spaces. Four bar stools sit on the side of the living room, opposite of the stove/cooking space, currently where I'm sitting with a great view of my husband's butt. I like how it looks in his well worn novelty boxers. They're patterned with his favorite video game character. It's a work of art.

Despite his lack of cooking skills, Lucas is very proud of his kitchen set up. He installed a hanging pot and pan rack to the ceiling, and several infomercial kitchen gadgets to "aid" in his craft. One of those slap choppers, an intricate veggie peeler, and even one of those small high speed blenders that fitness influencers push on social media. He never starts small with new hobbies. Cooking being his most recent. Last year, it was break dancing, and before that it was painting. He's had many others before these as well. The collection of his hobbies have since either become mementos on our bookshelves or clutter in our bedroom closet. Oftentimes, his mementos are his talking pieces when he brags and reminisces on his accomplishments at our gatherings, parties, or dinners. I was usually the cook of the home previous to this. So, if he chooses cooking isn't for him, hey, it's either more kitchen toys for me or a husband that cooks every other night. It's a win/win.

He speaks to me while facing the stove, eyes locked on to what he's cooking. "You're awfully quiet this morning. You feeling okay, honey?"

"Ehhh, I'm just… Maybe a bit fatigued. Maybe a little burnt out from work… Did you sleep well?" My throat has phlegm in it again.

"Yeah, I slept great. The hay rolling was fun this morning! Unexpected, but I'm certainly not gonna complain about it. Good way to start a Tuesday morning." he said. The pan and spatula continued to scrape and resonated through the kitchen. "Maybe you're sick from what you ate last night? That lo mein looked a little sketchy. Some of those noodles had a weird green tinge to them. That place also had mold on the ceiling, you remember that?."

"Yeah, the place was a little weird, but my stomach feels fine… I don't know… Could I have another coffee?"

"Absolutely. One sec, I'm just about done plating this."

He's frantically scraping the pan at this point. Sounds like another scrambled over easy egg. He turns around with a jokingly nervous smile and sets my plate in front of me. I was right. A botched egg, burnt bacon, and toast soaked in bacon fat with the carbon from the bacon glittered the surface of the toast.

"One of these days I'm gonna get it. I can make you something else if you like?" he offers as he hands me a cup of coffee.

I set the mug down and put on my best cute smirk as I pick up my fork, twirl it in the air beside my head, and land it straight down in a loose piece of egg. The tip of the fork swoops into my mouth, along with the egg. I slowly remove the fork from my lips and my eyes gaze up as if pondering my opinion. It's quite honestly the most rubbery egg I ever tried to chew on, but he doesn't need to know that.

"Mmmmm! Delicious! Bravo!" I cheer as I softly and rapidly clap my hands.

His smile is so precious. When I first started dating him, I was obsessed with how his eyes smile when he grins.

"I love you" he says.

I smile back at him and respond "I love you, too."

9:56 am

The elevator dings and the doors separate revealing my usual office space, a view that I see every day… and seemingly until I die, forever. My coworkers pace around trading papers and talking over each other as if it's a choreographed dance around the cubicles. The hum of fluorescent lights is the grand musical score of this ballet.

I walk past the meeting room with the whiteboard in the back of it listing objectives such as "RESTOCK STAPLES"or "quarterly reports due tomorrow at noon. sandwiches will be provided for hard

15

work" in all lower case letters. I then remembered that I shouldn't have brought my lunch today.

One of my coworkers approaches me.

"Good morning, Mrs. A—Aalders!"

"Jesus Christ, Nick, again, just call me Laura. You don't have to suck up to me."

"Thank you Mrs. Aal- I mean, Laura."

This almost child is Nick. His frame is tall, skinny, and he carries a slight hunch on his shoulders. It's his first week working for this company. Nick practically just got out of high school. He's nineteen and one of the references on his resume was literally his own mother. I ended up calling her to satisfy my sense of humor and curiosity. Turns out she's a sweet woman who raised a well-mannered son— from what I've seen of him so far.

I work in advertising. One of those agencies that designs billboards. More specifically, the company I work for owns almost half of the billboards in our city. It's easy money aside from maintenance of those things and a hefty liability and health insurance premium each month for the people that climb high ladders to put the ads up. I run a lot of the numbers that people below my position toss up to me, I summarize those numbers, then I toss those numbers above me. Numbers, numbers, numbers.

As of right now, I don't have Nick filling out any real paperwork or invoices. More so just organizing those previously described documents, small tasks with IT, and maybe an occasional coffee run. You could actually call him an intern, but I feel that's a bit too degrading and I prefer to make sure he gets paid well enough. He sort of reminds me of my little brother.

"What do you want me to get started on today?" He asks, looking at me with nervous anticipation, I can see his chest heaving and his face flourishing the slightest shade of pink on his cheeks.

"Give me just five minutes for me to sit down and settle and I'll come find you. Looks like you could use a breather anyway, Nick."

"Thank you, ma'am," he responds and I cringe.

I hate it when people refer to me as "ma'am". It makes me feel old. I'm only twenty-eight, god damn it.

I weave through the hectic bodies and make my way to the back where my small little office resides. It's nothing to gawk at. A small eight-by-eight space with filing cabinets, my pre-owned wood desk, vintage wood paneling surrounds it, and fluorescent lights occasionally flicker above me. My boss swears that my office "will be the next space to get rehabbed". I'd believe him if he clarified that statement with "in five years", since that's about when I'd guess he'd get around to doing that. His office was the first to get rehabbed to a modern white dry-walled space. Then the big modern office space I walked through previously got its own contemporary face lift. Mine is the only one still from the 1970's. Thankfully, my paycheck is good enough for me to not really give a shit, about sixty-five thousand dollars a year. I set down my laptop bag on the floor next to my desk along with my old red insulated lunch bag, and my steel coffee cup on the far right corner of my work space. As I'm pulling my laptop out of my bag I hear a knock at my door.

"Come in!"

My boss peers his head around the door as he opens it.

"Hey, good morning, Laura. How are you doing today?"

"I'm doing well, Mr. Linkzy, how are you?"

"Doing better now that the sun has risen. The view from this door is spectacular." His words make my shoulder muscles contract.

Even though I've barely glanced at him since he came through my door, I can feel him staring at my breasts as I'm bending forward in my chair to unpack my laptop.
He's really leaning into it early this morning. This creature of a thirty-eight-year-old man usually doesn't start saying this stuff to me until around lunch time when you can smell the whiskey on his breath more easily. His appearance is almost always that of a slightly tinted yellow button-up shirt that rests on his shoulders a bit too large, maybe he only owns one of them. It smells like it. He's like a small boy wearing his first suit. On his best days, his face is irritated from a presumably dull razor, but usually he just carries himself with generally poor hygiene. His body odor is just slightly stronger than the cologne he drenches himself with.

"I'm looking forward to your papers this afternoon. I'm even more so looking forward to the sandwiches my dad bought for all the hard work everyone has been showing. Especially you." he says.

"I never took you as a numbers person, Paul. You can't be that excited about my papers."

"Now, now. Remember, it's 'Mr. Linkzy' to you. Can you say that for me?"

Remember how I said it's easy for me to ignore the state of my office because of my salary? This part is not so easy.

"Yes, Mr. Linkzy."

"Good girl," he responds. My stomach lurches.

He turns around to leave the room and closes the heavy door behind him.

"Junior." I quietly call him, but he's already gone. I'd like to imagine he heard my defiance. He's only a shadow of his father, the one who owns the company I work for. The burning in my chest from my tiny act of rebellion is currently the only thing keeping me from imploding in my seat. I wish I was in the warm comfort of my bed and in Lucas' embrace. I want that more than anything at this moment.

12:03pm

The usual familiar faces and warm bodies shuffle into the conference room holding their laptops and papers. I'm already seated facing towards the city skyline with the table between it and me. Everyone clumsily seats themselves into the cushy office chairs and quietly mumbles about how fucked some of the numbers are this quarter. Once everyone is seated, Mr. Linkzy *Junior* walks through the door and sits to the left of the head of the table with the whiteboard acting as a backdrop. I swear you could see the green smell lines from here.

Lastly, Mr. Linkzy Sr., father of the company and his annoying twerp of a son, walks through the door. He's the only one in the room who carries a leather briefcase. He does not own a laptop, the calculators in his office are still analog, and the contrast between his modern office to his vintage officeware is stark and bizarre upon first noticing it. Linkzy Senior is top heavy with scrawny legs, has a well-groomed strong mustache, broad shoulders, and a gruff tone of voice. The smell of cigar smoke is heavier than his son's stench, usually. He is in no way affluent, but he still hosts the company Christmas parties at his McMansion and enjoys over-sharing his negative opinion of his wife's spending habits while showing off his baseball memorabilia.

"It always has to be a designer piece. From what I understand, it's just the logo that matters, right? Do you know what the big deal is?" I remember him asking me. I told him he was asking the wrong woman. I don't quite understand the hype either.

Before Linkzy Sr. even sits down, he begins to speak.

"Well, as some of you might have noticed, we're not doing so well right now. We didn't quite reach our goal for this season in light of the big game last weekend, but Summer is almost here and I think we're gonna be getting requests from the usual beer companies to push for Summer beverage sales."

He finally reaches the head of the table next to his son and begins to unpack his briefcase. That day's fresh cigar, paper work, and a silver pen. He continues.

"Road trips and frat parties are about to explode amongst the college kids, so we need to adjust our ad space prices for the boards along the highway closer to the colleges."

As he sits, he picks up his cigar, unwraps it, clips the tip, and toys with it in his hands as he gathers more of his thoughts.

"Make sure to push those to the alcohol beverage companies on some of your calls with them. Steve. Josephine. Marcus. Are you getting all this down?"

It's at this point, as if re-enacted from his favorite 70's mob film, he puts his cigar in his mouth and lights it with a match from his coat pocket.

"Yes, sir." one of them quietly affirms.

He pauses for dramatic silence. I swear, this man thinks he's an actor, but he would've made a half decent one if he had chosen that path from the beginning instead of advertising.

"Kyle. Other Marcus. Tom. Last year you all had a stellar idea of pushing our lawn care ads onto boards closer to the suburbs out West of the city. Do that again."

Another "Yes, sir." is heard once more. I'm pretty sure it was Other Marcus trying to stand out.

He takes a short puff of his cigar and groans the smoke out of his mouth before continuing.

"As far as I'm concerned, unless anyone else has any other ideas, the rest of our spaces can be just filler."

The room stayed quiet. No one had any ideas.

"Great," he says, and his face turns to that of disappointment. At that moment, you could tell the little director in his brain just called cut. If I were on his stage, the cameras in his mental film set would've had a more favorable light than my coworkers.

After the meeting, we're all lined up among the two fold-out tables holding accouterments and ingredients for sandwiches. White and wheat bread, beef or turkey, lettuce, tomato. Mayo and mustard packets from the break room. There's also a wholesale-size box of chips, with a number of various different flavors to choose from. The usual choices such as barbeque, sour cream and onion, cheddar, and sea salt. I'm starving and salivating at this basic buffet since, admittedly, I didn't eat much of Lucas' attempt at breakfast. I was too busy eating up his adorable smile. I craft myself a turkey sandwich and some barbeque chips. Rather than eat with my coworkers, I decided to eat alone in my office. I'm still a bit tired from this morning and I'm starting to feel the consequence of 3am sex and cheap American Chinese food from last night's dinner.

I enter my office, close the door, and sit down with my paper plate of food. I take the top slice of bread off the sandwich and start to add my mayo, and mustard, then I reach into my purse and grab a seasoning salt packet. I fucking love these things and they're the best invention since sliced bread. I then open my bag of barbeque chips, and try to fit as many as I can onto my sandwich. About 4 or 5 chips. I squish it down, lift up my masterpiece and go in for my first bite. Fucking. Immaculate. Ten out of ten. Laura Aalder, you've done it again. As I chew, the white bread becomes sweeter and the turkey, seasoning, and mustard come through. I needed this. It feels like a hard earned reward. I could melt into my seat. It's nearly intoxicating.

I hear knocking at my office door. God damn it.

"Come in!" I yell with my mouth full.

The door slowly opens and Linkzy Jr. comes in. Double god damn it.

"Hey, I saw that you weren't in the break room with us and wanted to check in on you. Are you okay?"

He's staring at my breasts again. I swallow my food to properly respond.

"Yeah, I just wanted to eat alone. I'll see you all after lunch."

He closes the door behind him.

"You know that Nick kid you hired? The short skinny lookin' kid?"

"Yeah, what about him?"

"So we noticed he doesn't really do much aside from cleaning, organizing, and a few other menial things. When will he start pulling his weight? It's been buggin' my dad watching him run around like a fairy."

Here we go. Defend him, damn it. Defend your decision. Defend yourself.

"Yeah, I'm just having him do small things first. More so to observe the work environment, catch how our financial rhythms go, and learn where everything is and the intricacies of this place. Getting him familiar with the small details. I think then he'll be ready for phone calls with previously established clients fairly soon."

"The small details?" he asks.

"The small details."

Linkzy takes a deep breath and puts his hands in his pockets on his exhale.

"Weeeell, alright. I suppose that makes some sort of sense."

Thank fucking god.

"However."

Fuck.

"Have you seen how he's been looking at you lately? Pure fuckin' puppy dog eyes on that kid. It's like he thinks you're his mama."

"Yeah, he's timid, but he's young. He's got room to grow." I responded.

"You think he's a show-er?"

"What?"

"I know why you hired 'em," he says.

Gross. I see where this is going.

"You don't think he's gonna try and make a move on you? Teenage hormones and all that, and you have that husband, uhhhh, Logan, right?"

"Lucas."

"Riiiight, Lucas."

The old A/C vent becomes the loudest thing in the room for just a moment before he continues on his point.

"Listen, Dad wants the kid out. Money is tight as it is. Get his paperwork sorted and have him out by the end of this week. Maybe find something for him to do that no one else wants to. Cleaning the chemical closet, maybe? That alone would make hiring the little shit worth it in the first place."

He glances at the clock on my wall and back to me as he pauses for a moment.

"I think I'm doing you a favor asking for this. Stopping you from doing something stupid. Not that you have yet, but I see right through you. It's only a matter of time."

There's that feeling in my stomach again.

"Did I make myself clear?"

"Yes, Mr. Linkzy."

He does a double take and acts offended.

"I'm not quite sure I heard you, Laura. Please let me hear you say it again."

I speak louder just to get this situation over with. My palms feel sticky.

"Yes, Mr. Linkzy."

He leans over my desk towards me and I get a better look at the bad dental work done on his teeth as his mouth opens for the next sentence. His five o'clock shadow, as short as the hairs are, you can tell they're greasy with old sebum and there's bits of his sandwich still stuck to the corner of his lips.

"Slower.", he punctuates. He theatrically shows his teeth as he emphasizes the R in the word.

The room spins around me and a nervous nausea sets in.

"Yes. Mr. Linkzy."

Silence drapes over us like a cold bed cover and the light flickers like a blink of disbelief. Under its privacy, he leans towards me and speaks as quietly as a secret.

"I love it when you say my name. It turns me on."

His breath scrapes against my skin like steel wool and his stink fills my nostrils. I get a view of a tight space in his trousers and he leans back away from me. He straightens his back and now his bulge is all I can focus on. Right at the edge of my desk just in front of my sandwich about a foot or so away.

"See you after lunch, Laura."
He turns around and leaves the room.

Instantly, the air in the room feels less humid. I force myself to relax my jaw. I look down at my lunch and it feels tainted. I'm not hungry anymore.

I left work about an hour after my interaction with Mr. Linkzy Jr., An early departure. Before I left, I went to put the lunch I brought to work initially into the fridge for the next day. Some of my coworkers were still straggling around in the breakroom when I entered.

"Hey, Laura. Feeling better?", one of them asked.

"Um, not exactly. The sandwich helped, but I think I'm going to excuse myself today. I'm still feeling a bit fatigued. Tell Nick to do what he can to organize the janitor closet before he leaves today. Be sure he wears gloves for safety, okay? Maybe even a face mask."

"Yeah, sure," they respond. "Not a problem."

As I'm setting my lunch bag on the shelf in the fridge, Mr. Linkzy Jr. makes another appearance walking past the doorway in the hall, then quickly back steps back into its frame as I stand back up from setting my lunch down. I close the door of the fridge. He grins at me from across the room. There are those fucking teeth again.

"Hey, Laura. You feeling okay?", he asks me. He speaks to me like a child.

"I'm still feeling a bit off. I was just talking about leaving early."

He steps into the room and side steps to the side of the door frame.

"Oh, well I'd hate to see you do that, but if you're unwell, you're unwell. I understand, so take the rest of the day off."

27

From across the room, he scans me head to toe for a moment.

"I'm glad I was able to get a word in with you earlier. I feel so much better and more at ease, y'know? I know what I asked isn't an easy task, but you'll pull through. My dad and I notice and appreciate the efforts you've given our company the past few years."

His eyes scan me once more.

"Happy to help!", I responded. I weakly smile and turn back to pick up my work bag from where I had set it beside my feet.

"No, seriously, Laura. I feel so much better."

The room goes quiet and the ice machine in the freezer breaks the silence.

"Well, I'll see you tomorrow, Laura. Call me if you need anything.", he says as he turns around and leaves.

My coworker's whispers bounced down the hall as I left the break room after that. The words I could pick out from them were "her", "him", and "of course.". They slowly faded as the distance grew. I do what I can to swallow tears as I try to escape to the safety of the elevator. I press the ground floor button and the doors take their time closing, the old tarnished finish on them cuts off the tunnel vision I have aimed at the space of the office and I begin to ball my eyes out. *That fucking bastard.*

I've been in my bathtub since I got home. Lucas hasn't arrived from his job teaching yet. I've just been soaking in this epsom salt bath. The stink from my boss feels like it left scratches on my cheeks. The water feels a little colder than room temperature, so I lean forward over my legs to uncover the drain to make more room for hot water. I turn the faucet as far as it can go. My hand almost feels oddly sensitive from how wrinkly it is and how it grips the handle so well, but also how I can feel every wrinkle on my finger tips. A flow starts and after a moment or two, the water quickly goes from cold, warm, to hot, to searing. The steel of the faucet fogs from steam and starts to form a condensation.

As the routine I've been repeating for hours goes, once up to temp, I let the water burn my feet as it breaks through the surface tension of the cold water. I keep my foot under it as long as I can stand until I instinctively pull my feet away into the safety of the coolness in the back of the tub where I sit. I play with the stream of hot water with my fingers playing chicken with the heat. My eyes wince every time my fingers graze it.

As the hot water finally reaches my knees, then my thighs, the heat becomes too uncomfortable and I turn the water's temperature on the faucet back down to what feels comfortable. My shoulders start to sting from the sweat droplets forming on my sensitive skin and my body is noticeably more red. My skin is all too sensitive from soaking in this tub for five hours. I turn the flow of the water off.

It's then I hear the sound of keys jingling against the outside of the front door from down the hallway. My chest tightens instinctually at first. I'm still flinching from earlier. My instincts calm once I realize it's just Lucas. I can hear the door knob turn as his keys jingle against his jeans and travel mug. I can hear him as he begins balancing himself and he slides off his sneakers. They thud to the floor. His keys jingle a little more and hit his mug like a bell. His socked feet eventually putter down the hallway to the kitchen where he sets his things down on what sounds like a part of the counter.

"Hey, honey! Are you here?" he yells.

"Yeah, I'm in the tub."

"Oh! Uhhhh!" he hesitates.

The gentle prodding of his steps gets louder as he approaches the bathroom. He walks in and scans the scene.

"Did he do it again?" he asks softly.

"Yeah…"

I stare down at my lap and lose where I am for a moment.

"Do you wanna eat dinner in here or out there?"

"In here."

"Oh…"

I hear him swallow and glance down at the floor as he turns his body out the door.

"I'll heat up some leftovers."

As he leaves I straighten my legs back out from their criss-cross position and I bend my knees up to where they're breaking the surface of the water. I let my torso sink in. I inhale deeply, puff my cheeks, and submerge my head. The stinging on my shoulder subsides and my hair floats around my face, grazing my cheeks. As if my body is automatically washing my boss' breath off for me, like it just knows what I need and how gently I need to be treated. I feel a little bit cleaner.

Lucas is sitting beside me with his plate of leftover chicken and mashed potatoes set on the lid of the toilet bowl, and scarfs a few bites down before he turns to me. I've been timidly eating off my own plate, which is sitting on the rim of the tub. Lucas wipes his mouth of chicken grease and continues to speak in a softly hesitant, yet slightly enthusiastic tone like his voice is gently nudging my spirit forward.

"So, basically, his wife could probably get you a spot in their advertising department. You know these journalists are all about ads these days."

I'm still staring at my lap.

"Laura?"

"I heard you. If her work has a better insurance plan, maybe. The thing is my job has that really good maternity leave policy." The weight of this hangs in the air for a second, this new chapter.

"Yeah, I remember, but you have to remember that I've been saving up a bit of cash from working overtime. If we get you a job with a policy that supports us a little less, I have money saved to account for it. We'll be fine, the baby will be fine, and you'll be safe."

"I don't think I like that risk. What if something goes wrong at the hospital? Like what if they need to do emergency surgery?"

I push a piece of the chicken sitting on my plate to the side, timidly playing with my food, and speak more.

"What if our baby ends up suffering from something like a sickness or defect?"

"Laura, you're overthinking this. Whatever happens, we'll be fine. I love you. I'm here to make sure you're safe and supported. You and our baby. You've done this for me in the past and it hurts to see you suffer from what you saved me from."

"These are different circumstances, Lucas."

"But they share the same solution."

I put a small dollop of mashed potatoes in my mouth and squish it with my tongue against the roof of my mouth. It's over-salted.

"I need time." I responded.

"Time?"

"Yeah, time."

"How much?"

"I don't know. I don't know if I can face it just yet. Work is busy as it is and I hardly have time or energy to draft a resignation letter."

His head refrains back as if I'm missing the obvious.

"We have time right now! Here let me go grab my laptop."

He stands up and scurries out the door for a moment and returns with his work laptop. He opens it up and clicks a few buttons to open up a document program.

"You speak, I'll type," he says.

I smile at him and take a breath through my nose. He mirrors me.

"You got this."

I begin to speak.

"Dear, Mr. Linkzy Sr. I regret to inform you that I've decided to put in my resignation papers and give four weeks notice" I begin with.

He starts clicking his keyboard into a fire storm with a smile on his face. He's proud of me and I'm thankful for him. I don't know where I would be if I didn't have his supportive nature in my life.

3:16am

Noise. It's silent but somehow there's noise. Like a hum. It's loud. I'm drifting forward and my vision is slowly pacing itself ahead of me. Clouds of pink, beige, and lines of red prance around my view as my eyes turn to and fro. My mental imagery draws pictures of myself watching news on the television. Stories of war across seas, fires burning in forests and homes. Women and children screaming for mercy. Families dragged out of their homes begging for just one more month to catch up on payments. The warmth of my body intensifies and it burns. I'm angry. I don't like what I'm seeing. My hands and feet are clammy, my teeth are gritting. All I can hear is what can best be described as chewing on fingers. Breaking the bones in the back of my molars, grinding them into jelly and bone meal. Before I can wince at how my stomach is churning, the sound of a man screaming angrily assaults my ear drums. The sides of my head where my ears are begin vibrating from its loudness. I finally realize I can move. I shoot myself forward and open my eyes. I scream.

"*No! Get away from me!*"

My eyes open already adjusted to the darkness. I'm still in bed staring at the open door of our bedroom. There's nothing down the hallway. I'm home. I swear to fucking god someone just screamed at me. Right next to me. Directly into my ear. My ears are ringing from it. I look over to my left and I see my husband still fast asleep clearly in a much happier dream.

Everything is as I left it before bed. The door is positioned as it was, my purse still on my bedside table, my oversized shirt is still on and covering me. Maybe it was just a dream. Obviously, there's no sign anybody was in here besides Lucas and I. I don't want to wake him up for nothing.

I lay myself back down and tightly secure myself under the now cold blanket and my body heat slowly brings it back up to warmth. I fall into Lucas' space and move his arm around my side. He's not exactly spooning me, but this'll do. I close my eyes.

"You know, that sounds like Exploding Head Syndrome."

"What?"

Lucas finishes chewing his waffle and swallows. He repeats himself.

"I said, 'I think that sounds like Exploding Head Syndrome.'"

"What the fuck is that?" I say as I chew and continue. "What a violent name. Christ."

"It's like, a kind of sleep paralysis, but instead of seeing a demon in the corner of the room or something, it's like, you hear a really loud noise instead."

He reaches over for his phone.

"One sec." he says as he unlocks his phone and starts typing away.

I'm still confused about the name 'Exploding Head Syndrome.' He begins to read off his phone.

"The National Institute of Health says, 'Exploding head syndrome is a benign, underdiagnosed sensory parasomnia. It is the sensation of hearing a loud sound during sleep-wake/wake-sleep transitions.'"

"So, I was just hallucinating?"

"Yeah, it seems so. Which makes sense because you've been under a lot of stress lately."

"Does stress cause hallucinations?"

"Makes sense though, right?" he asks

I take a moment to digest the name of this condition further. Is this a condition?

"Where did you even hear about this thing?", I ask him.

"I saw it on a short while I was doing my usual doom scrolling on social media. It was like 'Top 10 Unexplained Medical Phenomena.'"

I shake my head. Of course he would hear something like that from a fucking short or video or whatever it's called.

"Let me see your phone."

"Sure."

He passes me his phone and I scroll down the medical page for possible causes. It reads "Medications, stress, monthly cycle (usually right before a period)"

"Medications, stress, monthly cycle. Usually before a period.", I repeat off the page aloud.

"Well, at least we know now that the next pregnancy test is gonna be negative."

"Yeah, I suppose so, but it's not guaranteed."

"Fingers crossed", he says.

As I hand his phone back to him, part of me is glad Lucas decided to heat up some frozen waffles this morning. My appetite is back and I don't think I could force another rubbery egg down my throat again, but at the same time, the tone this morning is slightly somber in light of yesterday, and it's less exciting. I wanna see him smile.

I lean over towards him and grab his head. I pull the side of his face towards me and give him a big, wet, sloppy, gross, dramatically gregarious kiss onto his cheek.

"Ahhhhhhhh!" he exclaims!

"Thanks for breakfast, goober!"

I quickly jump out of my seat and hurry to the bedroom to get ready.

"Oh no you don't!", he yells as he chases me down.

"Ahhhhhhh! Don't eat me!", I playfully shrieked.

He grabs hold of me and collapses on me as we both fall into the bed. He pushes his lips onto my cheek and commences a wet raspberry. His spit is splashing into my shut eyes.

"No! Get away from me!" I feigned.

"That's what you get for getting my face wet!" he yells. He gets back up and hurries into the bathroom to avoid further childish conflict. Presumably to get ready for work.

I fucking love this dork. He's gonna make a great dad.

12:12pm

I've decided to stay in the break room for lunch today. Surrounded by my coworkers. I'll be fine if Junior makes his appearance this lunch hour, but I will not be caught alone with him whatsoever. Yesterday's encounter was really bad as it was. I don't need to spiral further. Especially since I made the stupid decision to wear a skirt today. It rests just above my knees.

Today hasn't had a great start. Upon arriving, I heard that Nick almost had a bad accident before I arrived today. He reached too high on the shelf in the janitor closet and almost had a whole open container of bleach spilled onto him. He's fine, but his arm got bleach on it and he was slow to wash it off so it got red.

How that closet is such a mess and why we have so many cleaning supplies, I have no idea. We haven't had a dedicated janitor since about two years ago, but still to this day Mr. Linkzy Sr. has Other Marcus run to the department store for more cleaning supplies every week or so. Just another one of those idiosyncrasies that people tend to have, I suppose. Everyone has a quirk or two, Senior asking for cleaning supplies is one of his.

The interesting thing is, he routinely hires a rotating selection of different cleaners to clean after closing instead of what we had before, so is he just being nice and supplying them with cleaning material? What's strange is I know cleaners usually bring their own. One of my close friends makes decent money cleaning rich people's homes. Maybe Senior is just that particular when it comes to his taste in chemicals? Is it just cheaper that way? You'd think I'd have numbers on that, but I do not. Maybe a business tax deduction for him.

Anyways, the second thing that happened today was that my lunch was missing. Not just the food, but also my precious red fabric lunch bag. I've had that thing since college. That bag had lasted me through so much, I'm really sad to see it go. I'd understand why someone would want to eat my lunch— until they realize Lucas cooked it, but to take my lunch bag too is pretty fucking ridiculous. Whoever took it, I hope they get stuck in our old elevator. *Asshole.*

With all of the leftovers from lunch yesterday, I managed to throw together a halfway decent backup lunch. I made myself a roast beef and cheddar chip sandwich with extra mustard. It's delicious. Junior hasn't come in for lunch yet, so I'm savoring each bite while I'm comfortable. God forbid I sink into my seat and get eye level with Junior's crotch. As of right now, Marcus and Tom are doing their routine venting about their phone calls.

"— and then he fucking hung up! That fucking prick!"

Tom balls his fist and hits it against the table.

"Yeah, that guy shouldn't have said that to you. That was uncalled for, but could you not spill my soup? You hit the table and just spilled it."

"Sorry, man. Paul's just been on my fuckin' ass about 'Oh, your call lengths are short and you're not retouching our call lists as quickly as expected of you, so what are you doing inbetween calls?'... Fuckin' dick, dude."

"Yeah. Ever since Mr. Linkzy saw the quarterly report, he's been screaming in his office on the phone with someone or whoever. I'm sure Paul is getting residual anger from his daddy behind closed doors."

"Doesn't mean he has to take it out on me, man!"

Tom doesn't even know the half of it.

3:00pm

The light above is me flickering again. I blink a few times to adjust my eyes. The flashing light around the blue glow of my laptop's screen is disorienting. I lean back in my chair trying to release the tension in my head that I've had from forcing myself to focus on numbers. Numbers, numbers, numbers. I reach over to my travel mug sitting on the far right side of my desk. I take a sip and this morning's coffee has turned cold, thick, and sweet with sugar. I reach over my laptop and set my mug back down on the far left side. It coats the roof of my mouth and it makes my coffee breath more noticeable. Of course, since my breath is bad, I need gum. Can't have anyone smelling my coffee breath. I reach down for my bag and begin to dig for my pack of mint chewing gum. Taking out the tattered paper package, I open it to find that it's completely empty.

Fuck.

"Mints", I remember, in the break room. I get up, leave my office, run down the hall and scan the break room for a mint. The jar is sitting on top of the fridge. I reach up, open the jar, take out a mint, unwrap it, and plop it in my mouth. Now my coffee breath is coated with minty breath.

Success.

Now I have to pee. Okay, okay, okay. One trip to the bathroom then I'm back to looking at numbers. Numbers, numbers, numbers. I run further down the hall past Junior's office and through the door just past it and into the bathroom.

Finally.

I pull my skirt up and sit myself onto the cold toilet seat. The need to pee is gone, so I try to push something out. Literally anything just to make this trip to the bathroom not in vain. Finally, a stream starts to fall and splash into the water. Once I finish, I wipe, get up, put my skirt down, and step forward to wash my hands. The soap burns a little since my hands are dry. I just know they're gonna be more cracked once I dry them. For a moment, I considered turning the water temperature up. I need to do something. I turn the knob further and steam begins to float out of the sink. I poke my finger under the running water and I hold it there for as long as I can. One second. Two seconds. Three seconds. I pull away. I inspect my finger and it's gone bright pink. I take a deep breath, turn the water off, and take my time drying my hands with a paper towel.

Once I finish, the light above me starts to flicker once or twice. Oh, maybe it's a power surge. This building is old after all.

As soon as that thought finishes, the room falls dark and I begin to panic. The residual heat in my hands quickly fades away.

Fuck, fuck, fuck. Where's the light switch?

I feel around the wall for approximately where I remember the light switch being. My hand grazes along the wall as my fingers scan for anything that isn't flat. My pinky catches the switch and I flick it down and up several times to test to see if that does anything. After a few flicks, the lights click back on. As soon the space gets brighter again, I turn to look in the mirror and see my reflection once more.

There's something off… There's no real noticeable change to my appearance, but there's something about how I'm looking at myself. Or rather, how my reflection is looking at me. It's still me. I am it, and it is me. It moves as I move and I move as it does.

"I know you're stressed, but you haven't let much of anything stop you from doing your best. You have so much love for yourself and your husband. All

you gotta do is stare at a few more numbers for two
hours, and time will fly right on by."

I finished speaking and the words that flew so
effortlessly out of my mouth inspires me and refills a
sort of resolve meter in my brain. I'm right. Just two
more hours and I'll be home to have dinner with my love
in no time.

Piece of cake.

6:00pm

"The basics, I'm just starting out with the basics.
Tonight, it's roasted carrots, potatoes, lemon parsley
scallops, and brown rice with a pan sauce." he says as he
cooks in front of me. The kitchen is smokey and thick
with burning oil.

Oh, great. Tree bark, rubber, and styrofoam
pellets.

"Yeah, that sounds great, honey!" I responded.

As he continues to click, clack, and bang pots,
pans, and baking trays together in his flow of culinary
exploration, I continue typing away on my laptop trying
to focus the noise he's making out of my already split
attention. I focus in. Marcus asked me to run over some
numbers he gave me. He forgot to run them himself and
gave them to me too late in the workday, so now I have
to look over and revise his mistakes before the deadline
tomorrow. This happens every so often with most of my
coworkers, especially Marcus. I swear to god, the
incompetence is unfathomable.

"I'm trying really hard not to burn the food this
time, so I'm keeping the pan at a low medium heat, but I

42

still wanna see the butter bubble around the scallops. Searing it on high heat wasn't the right move last time."

"Uh huh."

I continue scrolling down the page. Where the fuck did Marcus get this result? Something isn't right. Where did this extra money come from? The usual amount we charge is about $2,500 and some tax, but this is astronomically high. Why the fuck did they pay $11,498.56?

Lucas opens the oven and excitedly giggles.

"Oh, man! These roasted vegetables are looking great so far!" he says.

"Yeah, cool." I say to the computer screen.

He closes the oven.

"Hey, honey. Do you know where the peppercorn container is? The pepper grinder is out of-"

"Lucas, I need you to shut the fuck up for one fucking second. I'm in the middle of something here."

"Woah, hey. Where the fuck did that come from?"

"I need to run over these numbers from Marcus and I don't need to listen to how you're burning dinner again."

Lucas doesn't respond and turns back around to finish cooking.

$11,498.56. $11,498.56. $11,498.56. What. The. Fuck. This cannot be right. We either overcharged this client, had an elaborate three-dimensional artistic ad that I'm not in the loop on, or… Things are dire. I quickly run my eyes further down the spreadsheet to skim more numbers. Small numbers, large numbers, suspicious numbers. Ten grand, seven grand, a usual three grand. What the actual fuck?

"Do you want me to pack this up for you?"

"What?"

"I'm already done eating,"

I pull my eyes away from the screen to see a full plate next to my laptop.

"No way you're already done eating. You haven't even plated the food yet."

"You've just been staring at that screen for an hour."

"What? No, I haven't."

"Yes. You have. You've just been looking at that screen and muttering numbers occasionally."

I take a look around the kitchen and see that his plate is indeed empty, but not only that, the dishes are already drying from their cleaning next to the sink. In fact, Lucas is already in his pajama pants.

"Oh, I'm sorry, honey. I guess time went by a little faster in my head. Is there anything left for me to do?"

"No."

"Oh, well I'll pack up the food myself. Don't worry about it."

"Okay, well, I'm going to bed."

"Okay, good night!" I say with a smile.

Lucas wanders off to bed.

The feeling of hunger starts to set in and I decide to take a bite of the scallops and as its flavors soak on my tongue, I smile.

It was delicious.

Chapter 4

Does Everyone Have A Hole?

3:33am

Ow.

Ow.

Ow.

As my consciousness moves forward in my
mind slowly, I feel as if I'm being pulled from one space
to another. My eyes feel like they're open, but all I see
is black. I think my legs are moving. My arms are
holding onto an object and I feel like my weight is being
supported by something. My body is up right and my
hair is swinging and brushing against my back. My skin
is warm and sticky. There's a sudden nervous hot
pressure in my abdomen. My consciousness fades back
into the recess of my mind.

6:30am

Lucas' alarm starts beeping and my eyes open
quickly. Somehow, I'm already wide awake. I lay there
motionless staring at the wall ahead of me as I lay on my
side away from him. I feel Lucas turn his body and reach
to turn the alarm off and he proceeds to take the covers
off to leave bed. Once he does, the back of my body is
also revealed to the cold air. After a moment, he speaks.

"Laura, what the fuck."

He breaks my spell of concentration that I had
on the fine textures of the paint on the wall.

"Huh? What?"

"Laura, there's bruises all over your fucking body."

I turn my body in his direction and rest my weight on my arm.

"What?"

"There's like, three on your back."

I take the rest of the covers off and look down. He's right. There's one on my arm, a few on each leg, and a bite mark on my shoulder.

"Did someone fucking bite you?"

"What the fuck? Did you do this?"

"No, I didn't. Laura, I swear to god."

"Who the fuck bit me?"

"I don't know! I don't know!"

We spent the morning calling the police and reporting a break-in with the arriving officers. There was no sign of forced entry, nothing was stolen, and all the windows and doors were locked. In fact, hardly anything was out of place. My purse was still on my nightstand. We couldn't give much of a statement. The police left us a card and told us to call if anything occurs.

Neither Lucas or I had time or the appetite for breakfast and we didn't speak much aside from a "have you seen my shoes?" from me and a "I'm heading to work now. See you later." from him. After work, I'm going to buy new locks and ask Lucas to help me install them, including security cameras for the living room and bedroom.

My body is sore and I want to drown myself in bathwater.

Obviously since my body decided to spawn a bunch of mysterious bruises all over the fucking place, I'm not wearing a skirt today. I decided to wear a button up and these great leggings that look like dress pants. If there was ever a time to be thankful for these pants, it's now, because the fabric is gentle on the painful bruises on my legs. It even has pockets. The slip ons are also comfortable as hell. I know it's cold outside, but somehow, the coffee in my mug is already cold. It was steaming when I came into the building's lobby. In fact it burned my lip. The world is out to get me, it seems.

As soon as I walk off the elevator into my work, it's mostly quiet. Most of my co-workers are preoccupied with their own work, but I hear a few whispers throughout the office for those that aren't. I notice the two Marcuses eyeball me as I walk by towards my office. It's then, Nick approaches me.

"Mrs. Laura! I finished organizing the cleaning closet earlier this morning. Is there anything else you want me to do?"

"Nick, I've barely just arrived, give me five minutes to settle in, okay? I'll find you."

"Yes, ma'am."

"Don't call me, ma'am." I command.

He looks at me puzzled.

"Um… Sure, Laura."

"Okay, cool. Great. *Thank yoouuu!"*

I move my body around him, lightly bumping my laptop bag into his side as I try to walk past.

"Oh, wait! Mrs. Laura!"

"Yes? What is it, Nick?"

"Mr. Linkzy Sr. offered to take us down the street to check out that new ice cream spot that just opened up sometime after work. You're gonna join us, right?"

I ponder for a moment.

"No, I don't believe I will, but that's awfully sweet of the old man."

"Oh… Well, I'll see you once you're settled."

"Thank you, Nick."

"Thank you, Mrs. Laura."

It's *"Mrs. Laura"* now? He really doesn't want to just fucking call me by my name, doesn't he? He *really does* act like my little brother. Fucking shithead. He's trying to make me feel old or some shit.

I toss my laptop bag onto my desk, throw my jacket over the back of my chair, and put my travel mug on the far left side of my desk. I did not bring lunch today. Lucas said he didn't have time to make me one.

I sit down, open my laptop and pick up where I had left off on Marcus' spreadsheet. $11,498, $5,751, $7,928. $25,177 in one week of payments from these clients. I don't think we've ever had these companies work with us before. I move my cursor over to my email and click "compose". "Send to marcus***@mailbox.com".

"I looked over your spreadsheet and there's an astonishing amount of money being charged to a number of these clients. I've highlighted the ones of concern. Please double check these numbers immediately. Thanks."

I lean back into my chair and rub my eyes. Fuck. Fuck. Fuck. Last thing Senior needs is some sort of fiasco with the IRS. Big guy would die of a heart attack if we overcharge clients like this by accident.

I ended up forgetting to check in with Nick.

6:45pm

It's been a little over an hour since our office and call lines closed, and I'm once again stuck sifting through the debris of Marcus' broken math and poorly built reports. Instead of going home to the distractions of Lucas, I'm choosing to stay here. I was hoping Paul or his dad would have reached out about these discrepancies by now, but maybe Senior is too busy and more than likely, I'm putting too much faith in Paul's work ethic.

Knock, Knock, Knock.

Someone in the office at this hour?

"Come in!"

The door opens, and it's fucking Junior. Catching me alone again. I really thought he'd be going to get ice cream with everybody else. Fuck, I thought he'd maybe even be home by now.

"Everything alright? You're making a face..."

"Oh, sorry. Yeah, I'm just surprised by you being here at this hour is all... Plus, my body is hurting pretty bad right now." I rub my shoulder to console the dull bruised pain.

"Was I too much?"

"What? What do you mean?"

He adjusts his collar and straightens his back.

"Right. Keep the work environment work-related."

He clears his throat and I look at him anticipating an expected innuendo or glance.

"Anyways, Marcus forwarded me the email you sent him about the charges we've been making to a handful of our clients."

"Yes! Finally! What's going on with that?"

He hesitates for a moment. It's rare to see him choose his words carefully.

"It's nothing to be concerned about. These were charged for specialty services we began providing to some friends of my dad."

"What kind of services?"

"Again, it's nothing to be concerned about."

Bullshit.

"You're laundering money for someone, aren't you?"

He leans over my desk towards me and plants his hands on the surface. The thud of his weight nearly knocked over my mug.

"Laura, you shut your fucking whore mouth. What's it matter to you, anyway? There's nothing you're gonna do about it. Especially after what we did last night, you don't have much leeway in regards to blackmail. Even if you had the competency for something like that"

"Wait what? What did you mean last night?"

"Don't you fucking act like you don't remember. You called me up to ride my dick after all these years. Saying, 'I've thought about what kind of man I've truly been desiring all these years. The kind that knows how to truly handle a woman.'"

"That's a really funny joke, Junior.", I scoff

His eye twitches and he snarls a few teeth.

"Obviously, you're the one joking here. You loved how you let me use my toys to hit you all over."

"Wait-"

"How badly did they bruise, actually?"

He grasps my left arm to try and roll my sleeve up, but I quickly pull away. His hand was warm, but as callous as sandpaper.

"Oh, so I *did* get you good."

Wait. No, no, no.

"Don't act shocked and drop your act. I always fucking knew you'd crawl your way to me begging for my fucking dick. It was fucking delicious having your legs wrapped around me while I held your body and had it bounce on my cock."

I'm going to vomit. I'm gonna fucking vomit. He's lying. Words, words, words. I need words. Say something, damn it.

The pressure in my chest finally releases like a gas pipe bursting. My clammy hands lay flat on my desk, sticking to the surface as if to give myself grounding and support. I stand up and finally release fury.

"There is absolutely no fucking way- absolutely. No. Fucking. Way. I would ever call you up in the middle of the night to have sex with you, Junior. You are an incomprehensibly repulsive excuse for a human being. You reek of last week's shit, your teeth are rotting. I wish you rolled over and just died alrea-"

He strikes me right across my face with an open hand and I fall to the floor. My head cracks through the cheap wood paneling and my vision spins around me.

"Nobody calls me 'Junior', you manipulative fucking slut! You're lucky I ever hired you in the first place! My dad would've fired you if it weren't for me! I kept you around! I made sure you got paid! As far as you should ever be concerned, I fucking own your tight little ass. You owe me everything. You owe me your cunt and you owe me your world until I become your world. You will always be below me. You will never be free from the space under my foot. Do you fucking understand me?"

I can't speak. I'm so dizzy. Adrenaline has numbed the pain in my head to a tickle and I'm trying to uncross my eyes. I can't breathe and my lungs struggle to grasp onto a natural rhythm to breathe to.

"Do you fucking understand me, you bitch? Huh!? Do ya!?"

"Paul, please stop.", I try to cough out.

"Call me, Mr. Linkzy!"

I can't speak. All I can muster is a wheeze whistling through my throat.

"Paul, please, I'm sor-"

"Say it like you say it to my dad!"

He kicks me in my stomach. I vomit into the crumbs of the wall surrounding my head and it trickles onto the collar of my shirt. The air trapped in me gets pushed out by his foot, and I can finally gasp for air. My vomit goes down my windpipe and the acidity of it burns. My body is only allowing my body to cough. I don't know how to break the spell of it. I can't stop.

"Fucking say it, Laura. Fucking say it!"

I still can't form a word as I'm still coughing out what I can of my vomit. It tastes like the snack from the vending machine I had earlier. He kicks me again, this time at my chest. I gather all my nerves to attempt to utter one word.

"Yes…"

"Yes, what?"

I pause another moment to utter more words to work up a satisfying response to get out of this situation.

"I'm sorry, Mr. Linkzy."

I can't breathe.

"Say it again."

I hear his belt unbuckling and his pants unzipping.

"Fucking say it again." he reiterates agitatedly.

The pressure in my chest is unbearable. My face tightens as tears force their way from the corners of my eyes. The room spinning and the tears turn my vision into a kaleidoscope of fear.

"I'm sorry, Mr. Linkzy."

I try to push myself up to try and release my head from the hole in the wood paneled wall, but he puts his foot on me and forces me down. He begins to masturbate over me.

"Say my dad's name again. Like you were last night."

This can't be real. This has to be a nightmare.

"C'mon. I know you can do it, baby girl. You did it so much for me last night. This is what you wanted, right? What you asked for over the phone? Just fucking say it."

The sound of his flesh clapping has my head contract between my shoulders.

"I'm sorry, Mr. Linkzy."

"Yeah, keep going, you dirty whore." he continues.

I'm sobbing. I haven't had a solid breath of air and my body is demanding for more oxygen as this continues on. Every hiccup I make while hyperventilating burns my insides and my hands claw at my chest. A faint attempt at a scream frees itself within me.

"Please, let me leave, Mr. Linkzy!"

"Not yet! One more fucking time!"

"I'm sorry, Mr. Linkzy! I'm sorry, I'm sorry, I'm sorry!"

He finishes and I feel the weight of it fall on my shoulder. He takes his foot off me as he zips his pants. He takes a step back and composes the pace of his breaths. I can smell his whiskey breath from here on the floor.

"See? Wasn't that fucking hard was it?" he pants.

I can't formulate a sentence to respond. I'm at the mercy of the grip my muscles have over my bodily control, but my vision clears and I become less disoriented.

"Don't ever fucking forget this. You're my bitch and you always will be. I had you swinging around my body like you were on a stripper pole. We basically bumped into everything in my apartment last night and I know eventually, with time, you'll want more. You have a need for medicine for a sickness in your soul, and letting me cum inside you is your dose."

As he leaves, he spits on my leg. Once he closes the door behind him, my hands tighten into

white-knuckled wrecking balls and my sobs break the
mental dam of my restraint.

*I fucking hate him. I've never hated anyone more
than anything in my entire existence. Everything inside
of me is burning. I wish that monster was dead. Fucking
dead that piece of shit. That fucking asshole cretin
mother fucker. I want him burning and his head melting
on a pyre in front of the whole world. I want everyone to
know that his putrid existence is not worth tolerating any
longer. Not with my future children around. I don't want
him to hurt them or Lucas. That son of a fucking bastard.*

I use my anger as an energy to attempt to push
myself up off the floor again. The smell of my own
vomit finally hits my nostrils and the sensation of bits
from the wall stuck to my puke-covered face finally hits
me. I sit up and look down at the mess my head was in. I
move the hair that's stuck to my face out of the way. The
hole is about the size and shape of a fire hydrant. I look
at the rest of my body. My old coffee is spilled on the
carpet, there's an awful-smelling dirty glob of spit on my
pants, and my slip-ons are almost off. I'm a whole
fucking mess. My office is a mess. What am I going to
do? What the fuck happened? Did we?... I refuse to
believe it. I vomit in the hole Junior put me through.
Once I pull my head up from the hole, I finally do
believe it.

What Paul just now did to me… It isn't the first
time something like this has happened in my life. When I
was in high school, my first girlfriend put me through a
similar nightmare to this one. She was just as sadistic
and probably left more bruises on my body than Junior
did. Actually, she was more careful about where she left

them, too. I'm now revisiting that old hometown. Right now, I'm staring at the tree with a dark history hardly anyone but its victims talk of. My attention returns to the mess in this room.

I am never letting this happen again. I fucking swear on it. Never again.

"It's okay. Everything is going to be fine.", the mirror says. The lights flicker. "Just a few bruises."

I… I just couldn't go home. I couldn't face Lucas and tell him what happened at the office today. I don't have the strength to right now. He's been texting and calling me all night. Asking me where I am.

"You need time to build your strength, that's all. Your boss just beat you into a wall and it's a lot to unpack."

I wish my husband was holding me. Instead, I'm at a bar. One, of which, I do not know the name of. The menu just has items listed. When I left work, I just drove. I let the lines of the road tell me where to go– the street lights were a line of Northern Stars. I've been here all night drinking. Soaking my heart in sterile medicine with a cloudy shot glass. One shot, two shots, three shots. I did this last time this happened. Although, back then, I would sneak my parent's vodka into bottled sweet tea that I would then bring to school. One shot, two shots, three shots. Eventually, I was stealing bottles of vodka from the grocery store. Mixing different kinds of liquor together into an angsty concoction only a teenager could bear drinking. When I was alone at home, I would take a 16oz glass and fill it with half vodka or whatever and half fruit punch drink mix. I'd drink about four of those before passing out for the night. One shot, two shots, three shots. Eventually, I was able to just naturally stop drinking. The urge to purge went away, but resentment and cynicism settled at the bottom of the chaos I bottled up. Steeping in the essences of my soul. One shot, two shots, three shots.

I bring myself back from dissociation. I'm holding myself up over the sink. The sink shifts every time I lose my severely drunken balance. "FEAR" is written in all capital red letters on the bathroom stall and the walls are littered with various sigils, tags, words of encouragement, one liners, and obscenities of various forms— some hateful and foul. The white tile, slightly yellow, aged, and scum rests in the streak of the caulk between each small tile. My reflection carries an unfamiliarity. I can't tell if it's my vision that's blurry, or the reflection itself.

"You know Lucas. You'll explain everything when you get home. He'll embrace you with open arms once he knows you're safe.", I say to myself. My shoulders ease for a moment. My reflection interrupts.

"Do you think if you swung a machete hard enough that you'd have the physical strength to cut Paul's head off?"

"What the fuck?" I replied.

"Yeah! Think about it! Doesn't that sound like something worth thinking about?" It continues. "It honestly sounds fun. I wanna see the fucking piglet squirt hot red juices everywhere. That wholeheartedly evil man deserves to have his veins chewed open by disease ridden rodents."

"*Oh, fuck.* My stomach." I hunch over. The thought exasperates my nausea. I vomit into the sink what was previously vodka, but could now be considered something akin to bodily jungle juice.

"Look at you go! Get it all out of your system. You're doing so good.", I say to myself. My blood pressure spikes from heaving so hard and my ab muscles are twitching. My arms are weak and I shuffle my weight again. The alcohol in my blood spins through my head and my vision as I try to ground myself once more. I almost tore the sink from the wall. "Woah, that was a close one!" It continues. Don't fall over on me now. You just made more room for self-care. Can't you pass out now."

What?

"Yeah! Come on! We're gonna go drink some more! You need to have some fun! Loosen up a little."

"I don't think I could be looser than I already am. I need my husband.", I think to myself.

"Nonsense! C'mon! Let's go!"

As if pulled by string, my legs shuffle and carry myself forward toward the bathroom door. With my arms out in front of me as if I was the star of a ballet, I burst through the door with vigor and excitement and walked back to my barstool.

"Let me have uhhhhhh.", I exclaim with my lips gleefully stretching.

The bartender turns around as he adjusts his attention to me.

"Do you want another shot of vodka, ma'am?" he mutters.

"Oh my gosh! How did you know!?" I giggled. I push my arms on the bar and lift myself with my feet planted on the support beam, between the legs of the barstool. I lean my body closer to the bartender. I grin and bite my lip. "I love a man that knows what a woman wants."

4:00am

"He did what!?" Lucas is screaming. Confused, angry, scared, and protective. The loudness of his voice hurts my head. I don't know if his voice is shaking the part of my slight concussion to cause the pain, or the hangover taking shape. Maybe it's both. He's confused as to why I felt I couldn't bring myself to come home and find safety in his arms. He more than anyone in my life would be understanding of this victimhood I feel. He's angry at Paul for slapping me across the room into the wall and for masturbating over me. "I could kill him! I'll fucking kill him!" he yells into the air as he paces. I'm sitting in front of his storm. Front row seats. He's scared that Paul will do it again. Scared of what could've happened to me at the bar. Scared of what might happen if I continue working there, and scared of what he, himself, might do. Something that carries the consequences of jeopardizing his life and Paul's. "You need to leave that place immediately. You cannot— I cannot allow you to be in the presence of that man again."

"Lucas, I can't— just walk away from my job. I need to", I abruptly stop and struggle to continue as everything spins around me. The sentence claws its way out of me. "---to keep getting paid to keep a roof— over our heads.", I'm just barely able to get it out of my mouth. The muscles of my mouth trip over the words like cracks in the sidewalk. He stops pacing and quickly stares at me befuddled at my statement.

"What the fuck are you talking about? Laura, he slapped you into a wall, kicked you in the stomach, and sexually assaulted you. To Hell with working there! I have my savings to get you out. We need to file a police report!"

The residual influence of the vodka has my eyes relaxed and I'm dazed looking at the wall. My jaw is relaxed and I'm about to drool. The texture of the paint feeds my zombie-like demeanor. "I uhhh— can't walk away. Need— to—"

"God, you're a fucking mess." he walks over to hold me up. "Honey, look at me. Lock eyes with me." My eyes glaze through his for a moment until only glitters of my focus appear. "You need to get to bed. You're in no state to have this discussion. Come on, you're gonna have to help me here." He leans forward towards my abdomen and tries to pick me up over his shoulder like a firefighter rescuing me from distress. I do what my body can allow to lean forward over his back as he rests my arm around his neck and lifts me. He proceeds to carry me down the hall to our bedroom. My stomach is pressed against his shoulder and with every step he makes, it churns my stomach into nausea, but there's nothing to spill regardless. My whole body is sweating a fever out, as if fighting an infection.

"Christ. Did someone roofie you?" He gently sets me into bed and a giant blot of sweat is revealed as I'm peeled from his clothing.. "Sorry, honey. I'm not strong enough to hold you in my arms like a knight." he stammers worriedly. He takes off his t-shirt carefully to get the yuck off of him. My body is limp and I sink into the soft bed. He walks away for a moment and returns with a large mixing bowl lined with a plastic grocery bag and a wet rag. He sets the bowl down on the floor at my side of the bed and proceeds to wipe residual vomit flakes from my collar bone from earlier in the bar bathroom. He flips the rag over to a clean side and wipes sweat from my brow and cheeks. The rag is warm and considerate and it rubs against my cheeks and the corners of my mouth. He slips my slip-ons off and unbuttons my shirt. "C'mon. Sit up and let me get this off of you." He holds me up against his chest and my head rests on shoulder. As he struggles to pull my shirt off my arms, I feel that burning in my chest and pressure in my groin. Temptation takes the front row of my drunken thought process. I open my mouth and let my tongue out. I slowly drag it across the side of his neck. He stops what he's doing for a moment and pulls back. "Honey, now is not the time for that." I push forward to try and suck on his neck to sway his stance, but he holds me away and gets stern. "Seriously. You're drunk, sweating, sick, and barely conscious. Now is not the time for that. You need sleep."

"I need your coooo-ck." I complain. I whine and lay my back down onto the bed.

"Laura! Stop talking like that. It isn't cute. You're making me uncomfortable."

I comply and struggle to drag the shirt off my arms and throw it to the side. I remove my bra and set it in the same place. He's not looking at me anymore. He's looking at the bruises all over my body, in disbelief that they and I are of the same entity. The newest of my collection of purple blots being where Paul had kicked me. It's a giant amongst the rest of them. It's a deep sangria color, with tints of brown and dark orange surrounding the dark circle. Whatever has bled in me has settled, clotted, and stopped moving. It's like an eclipse.

"You're such a gentleman. It turns me on, I can't help it." I say sultry-like.

"Laura, seriously. Quit it. This isn't like you. You're under a lot of distress and you need sleep." He puts the blanket over me to cover his nightmare. He gets up and leaves again. "Be right back."

As I relax into the bed and my body slowly declares the spot home for the night, my focus shifts to the ceiling. My vision isn't running around as much as it was in the living room and my train of thought is getting clearer. I begin to reflect on the night. From the drive to the bar— and how the lines of the road guided me, to my time at the bar, my time with the bartender to skip the tab, my time with the taxi driver that drove me home with the free fare I was able to get, and finally the time I tried to have with my husband. My husband is as patient as a statue and vigilant on his values and morals. Always has been. It's not hard to appreciate how strong of a man he is, but frustrating how boring he can be. I'm consenting. I'm present. He's married to me after all. It's not a big deal. He's acting prude, but he's not boring. He's a challenge. I want to sink my teeth into him.

He returns with a tall glass of water and a bag of chips. "I have this water for you to drink and a snack to fill your stomach with something. Don't worry about puking it out later. It's better to puke something out than nothing. It's bad for you to puke nothing but bile."

I shift my eyes from the ceiling to look at him to reply. "I'm not gonna puke." I raise my eyebrow for a second.

"Laura, please listen to me. I really don't like how you're talking to me."

"What are you? A pussy?"

His glare goes from surprised to stern.

"I said no, Laura."

"Pffffft, fine." I say blow out my lips and stare at the ceiling again.

He takes a deep breath and speaks.

"I'm gonna sleep on the couch tonight. This whole situation… I'm worried for you. Please, feel free to sleep in and we'll talk more in the morning. I'll call in sick for you."

I stare at him with a blank expression. "Worried for me?" I think to myself.

 I'm gonna set an alarm to check in on you later tonight to make sure you're not choking on your vomit."

"I'm not gonna vomit." I reply

"You might."

"I won't"

"Laura, listen to me. I've been worried sick for you all night. You missed all of my calls and all my texts, then suddenly you burst through the door in tears and in a drunken stupor. I'm really not in the mood to argue and I'm certainly not in the mood to have sex with you. I just cleaned puke off of you. Get some sleep, I'll check in on you in a bit." He turns around, turns the lights off and walks through the door. "I love you. Sleep well." he says as he leaves the door ajar. It's dark in the bedroom and the streak of light from the hallway eventually goes out and I hear him shuffle onto the couch.

 Fucking asshole.

Lucas wakes up. "Wait, where are you going?", he says as his body shoots up from the throw pillow.

I'm already dressed. Same clothes from last night. Fake dress pants, button up, slip ons, but cleaned. As if there was never a mess to begin with. In fact, my coffee is hot and I have my lunch packed in a grocery bag. I'm walking towards the door to exit as I speak. "I'm going to work to turn in my resignation letter. There's still coffee left in the pot." He wasn't supposed to be awake yet.

"Resignation?" Lucas stands up and walks over to me and halts me. I turned around to him. "Honey, you need to leave that place. Who knows what could happen in the four weeks you'll be there? We also need to get the police involved."

"Lucas, it's better this way. If we start firing accusations at them, they'll lawyer up. We don't have the money, time, or resources for that. Plus, it's a bad look on my image for future employers. I've spent this long climbing the ladder, I can't have myself slip and fall from throwing accusations at former employers."

His brows furrow and his expression is confused. "So you're gonna resign, and work there as if nothing ever happened? How is Junior going to react?"

"Paul isn't going to do anything. He'll tease, and press, but I'm not going to allow him the liberty or satisfaction to get to me. Trust me." I can tell Lucas is extremely unhappy with my decision, but then his frustration pauses and he begins to scan me.

"When did you clean your clothes? Where's all the vomit and sweat? Aren't you hung over?" he wonders outloud.

"I couldn't sleep. I ended up just washing my clothes and finalizing the letter we wrote together."

"No, you didn't? I had been checking on you all night. You were fast asleep and still a wreck."

"Maybe you were just dreaming, Lucas. Otherwise, how could I have done all this?"

He stares down at the floor and I can see through his eyes that he's flipping through and trying his best to recollect his memory as if he missed a major detail. "Yeah, I guess… I guess I was dreaming." he gathers.

"You were dreaming." I conclude.

He takes a few more moments to digest the situation, but I haven't the time to watch his cute little confused face put the pieces together. "I need to go, Lucas. I'm going to be late."

"Okay." he says. He leans in for a kiss and I oblige. I kiss him and hold it to taste the moment and savor the scent. He pulls back. "I love you." he says.

"I love you, too, darling." I replied.

10:00am

The door to my office opens and Nick walks through. I'm seated at my desk with my hands clasped together. I've been patiently waiting for his arrival. He's pink and nervous. He's never seen my office before and I'm sure he's trying his best to figure out what the occasion is.

"Hey, good morning, Laura." he greets. "How are you feeling this morning? You look refreshed."

"Never better, Nick." I smile. "Please, take a seat."

"Of course."

He seats himself and notices the large hole in the wall. It looks like it had gotten a little bigger from when I was last in.

"Is that what we all heard the other day?"

"Nick, focus."

His attention is back to me and he stares intently at me. "Okay." he says. I take a breath and continue. The light flickers like a snake's tongue smelling the air. He still occasionally glimpses at the hole in the wall at my side.

"So, Nick. I won't waste my time getting to the point here. I've made the decision to let you go immediately. Please, pack your things and leave. You'll receive your last paycheck in the mail. It will not be direct-deposited."

"W-wait, what? Why?"

"I just don't believe I see you as a nice fit for the company's future. You're nervous, fidgety, and rude. It's not the quality service we want our customers to receive."

"Wait, fucking how? I cleaned that disgusting ass closet for you, I've run coffee so many times to the point of my white sleeves going brown, I've organized all of the invoices from the last five years, and that's how you see me? Laura, look at my arm! My arm is still peeling from the bleach that got spilled on me." He holds his arm up to my view.

"Then I guess you should've been wearing your brown sleeves, Nick. Could've killed two birds with one stone."

"What the fuck, Laura?"

"See, Nick. This is what I'm talking about. Unprofessional. Rude. Undedicated."

"Undedicated!?"

He pulls his body closer to the desk in frustration. He leans towards me.

"Did I stutter?" I quip.

Tears start to well his eyes and he sniffles pathetically. Poor fucking baby. It's a good thing he's got a sweet mother at home. He's gonna need to be cradled for a while.

"You're a fucking monster, you know that?"

"And Paul was right. You are a little shit. An ungrateful little shit who doesn't appreciate opportunities when they're presented to him."

"I've been doing nothing but chasing every single one you've given me."

"Oh, really? I never noticed. Do better next time."

"Fuck. You."

He stands up and turns around to leave.

"Good bye, Nick. Don't let the elevator eat you." He doesn't respond and slams the door behind him. My mug jumps slightly to the right on my desk. I move it back to the left. In its rightful place. I smile.

All in a day's work.

Knock, knock, knock.

"Come in!" I hear from the other side of the door. I open the door and I enter Mr. Linkzy Senior's office. His office reeks of cigars and his signature modern decor/vintage tools appear in my view. He's seated at his desk shuffling through his lunch container. It looks like a poorly made meatloaf. Disappointingly gray-ish.

"Oh, Laura! Wasn't expecting you in for work today. Please take a seat."

"Thank you, Mr. Linksy." I seat myself in front of him. My letter grasped in my hand.

"It's actually good that you came in just now. I had been meaning to check in on you. See if you're feeling better." He looks nervous. His skin tone is red and he begins to sweat a little.

"Uh huh." I replied. I handed him my letter. He reaches over his lunch and grabs it. He scans it for a few moments and he turns a little less nervous now. His red has turned to a pink.

"You're resigning?"

"Yes, Mr. Linkzy."

"Is… Is that all? Four weeks and you're gone?"

"Yes, sir."

"Oh…" He stares down at his lunch again, sighing a subtle breath of relief, but continues a nervous demeanor. Like my husband did this morning, his expression reads as if all the pieces of the puzzle were never meant to fit into one clear picture. "I uhh… I told Paul to stay home. He looked a little stressed from the recent work load I recently put on him. Silly me." He wipes sweat from his brow and puffs on his cigar.

"I noticed." I replied. I don't think I've blinked since I sat down moments ago. I've just been staring at him. Soaking in his nervousness and mannerisms.

"Are you okay, Laura? Anything you need to talk about?"

"I've never been better, Mr. Linkzy. May I go back to my office and finish my work?"

"Yeah, umm, of course. In fact, feel free to leave for the day. I'll have Marcus finish your work for you. I think it's about time he does a little bit of your work for a change."

"Thank you, Mr. Linkzy." I stand up to leave, but Mr. Linkzy calls for me.

"Laura?"

I stop and turn around to him.

"Yes, sir?"

"I saw the hole in your office wall. What exactly did Paul do in there with you?"

I turn to him once more and I say "Nothing, sir. We just talked."

"Talked?"

"Talked."

6:00pm

"Are you sure you don't want me to cook tonight? You've had an extremely rough time lately." Lucas says

"Nonsense." I responded confidently. "Afterall, I feel the need to thank you for treating me so well last night. You were such a gentleman. You cleaned my puke, put me to bed, kept me safe. I need to make sure my wonderful husband knows I love him."

"Whatever makes you happiest, my dear." he responds. The two New York strip steaks in front of me sizzle in the iron skillet. I cut a chunk of butter and dropped it in. It bubbles into a liquid, and once melted, I drop in sprigs of fresh rosemary and lavender. I begin to baste the steak in the infused butter. There are also potatoes and asparagus in the oven. The potatoes are seasoned classically. Salt, pepper, garlic powder. The asparagus, however, has a bit of a twist. It's seasoned the same as the potatoes, but they've been tossed in a light coating of dijon mustard prior to baking. They'll be receiving lemon zest once out of the oven. You practically smell every ingredient, every spice, every detail radiating from the food and throughout the apartment.

"Smells delicious, Laura. It's been a while since we'd had steak."

"Well, I was passing by the butcher on my way home from work today and I figured I'd pick something up as a celebration for dropping off my resignation letter to Mr. Linkzy today." I kick my heel up and scrunch my face into a cute expression towards him.

"Speaking of which, how did he take it?"

"Oh, he took it fine, he took it *fine*!"

"No mention of Junior?"

"Oh, he said Paul stayed home today. Felt under the weather. *Poor little man.*"

"Right." He looks at me worriedly. He gathers his concerns and speaks more. "Are you sure you're doing alright? You seem… Oddly peachy for someone who was assaulted yesterday."

I turn my head to him and my eyes dart to his. He flinches, almost as if I shot a laser at him from my eyes. "What do you mean, Lucas? I'm just processing it as I need to be." I asked him.

"Oh, by all means! It's great to see you energized, making dinner, getting shit done and all that, but… It's just unexpected of you, that's all."

"Lucas, the best marriages are the ones where you're constantly discovering new things about your lover despite being together for so long. I thought you of all romantics would know that."

"Sure, but that's not exactly what I meant." he adds.

"The important thing is that I'm happy. You do like that, I'm happy, don't you?"

"Yes, but—"

"But what, Lucas?" I say to him as I turn to him fully. My back is straightened and my chest is forward. He stares at me. He's scared. As he stares, his attention is then diverted to the pan smoking behind me.

"Laura, the butter is burning!"

"Oh my!" I exclaim as I focus back on the pan. I pull the steak and set it on the cutting board. As it rests, I remove the roasted vegetables from the oven and zest the asparagus with the lemon I set off to the side. I decide to talk to Lucas more to pass the time as the food settles. "How was your day, sweetheart?"

"Oh, it was fine. Most of the kiddos are having trouble with division, but it's like that every year."

"Yeah? Anything else?"

He ponders for a moment. I've noticed it's hard for men to talk about how their day was, but the key is patience… Or atleast in Lucas' case.

"Actually, there's this kid that keeps doing weird shit at recess. It's concerning some of the teachers and it's really hard to get in touch with some of the parents about his behavior."

"What's he doing?"

"Well." he pauses for a moment, trying to formulate his story. "He just… Keeps eating fucking bugs."

"Bugs? Isn't it, like, normal for kids to eat bugs sometimes?"

"Allow me to clarify. He actively searches and eats bugs during the entirety of recess. He'll shuffle through the mulch, dirt, mud, look under play equipment and just eat them. Like, obsessively. Other students have been either scared to play with him, or are torturing the poor kid during learning hours. They keep calling him 'monkey boy' and 'chimp'."

"Oh. Poor little guy. Does anyone know why he does it?"

"I mean… You remember Kathy, right?"

"Ms. Hendrix? Yeah, I remember her. She made that wonderful non-alcoholic mulled wine for the teacher's Christmas party last year."

"Yeah! Her!" he exclaimed. He continues.

"She pulled him aside to the pavement area one day trying to stop him from eating spiders under one of the benches, and out of a frustrated curiosity, she asked him why he chooses to spend his recess eating insects instead of playing with others?"

"Well, what did he say?"

"Supposedly, he said that he just loves them so much."

"As if he loves eating them?"

"No." he says. "As in he loves them so much, he wants them in him. As if he's keeping them in him forever. His binders, backpack, even some of his clothes are all bug related. He just really fucking loves bugs!"

"Oh." I quickly glance back at the food to check on them, then back to Lucas. "That's awfully… deep and spiritual for a kid that age."

"Yeah. I'm sure the kid is really intelligent. Sure has the empathy to prove it, but I don't teach him or grade him, so I can't say for sure."

"That is awfully odd."

"Yeah." he finishes.

I finally turn around to finish prepping the food for plating. I slice the steaks into thin bite sized strips, plate the veggies and zest the asparagus, and drizzle the pan butter over the steak. I present my work to Lucas.

"Holy shit, Laura. This looks delicious. You really outdid yourself this time!"

"Thank you, darling."

"Yours looks a little under done, though. You want me to nuke it for you?"

"Oh, no. I decided to cook my steak blue-rare tonight."

"Blue rare? But you always have it medium-rare."

"Well, I figured I'd try something new."

Chapter 7
Ugly Fucking Liars
10:00pm

I can feel my face glow a blue hue as I stare blankly at the television. I'm stuck on the couch and this glass of vodka is glued to my hand. I lift it and it touches my lips. One sip, two sips, three sips. I put my hand and the glass back on the arm rest.

"He texted me again," the blonde girl on the television says. "It's from 'B'." Shock, awe, suspense. It's been a long time since I watched this show. How the hell anybody in this show let this girl date her teacher, I will never fucking know. What a wild show to grow up with. At that moment of thought, Lucas walks out of the bedroom door, down the hallway, and approaches me from behind. I could hear his sock covered footsteps.

"Hey, are you coming to bed soon, honey?" he asks

"Yeah, after this episode." I take another sip from my glass.

I can feel him glance at my drink. "You picked up more of that today?" he asks.

"Yeah. The price was really good. You get a big bottle, too."

"Did you remember to get those security cameras from the store today?"

"Oh, sorry." I responded. "I totally forgot. I had to grab a few other things from there. Hair product, make up, some wipes, pregnancy tests. I guess I forgot to put that on my list." I still haven't broken my eyes away from the television.

"It should've been on your list two weeks ago," he argues. "And plus, drinking vodka on ice isn't gonna help with trying for the baby."

"I'll stop drinking when the result is positive." I react.

"Okay, well, are you pregnant?"

"No, but I'll test now. I could go pee."

"Thank you", he replies.

I set down my drink on the coffee table and pause the show on the TV. I grab the pregnancy test from the kitchen counter and make my way to our bathroom. I drop my pajama bottoms and sit on the seat, clumsily holding the test under me ready to have it catch my stream. I forgot to grab a cup. My pee finally releases and it sprays onto the test. I wipe, stand, pull my pants up, and set the soaked part of the test over the sink. I decide to flip through my phone as I wait. I scroll through social media and try to decipher the words through my blurred sight. Mostly just an endless list of headlines, so and so is now single, people from highschool on tropical vacations. So much nothing. Before I know it, minutes pass, and I look to check on the test. A cold wind goes down my spine and my body freezes. It's positive. All of a sudden, I'm hot and I can't look away.

You'd think I'd be happy. Elated, even. Lucas and I had been trying for a year for this to happen, but I'm scared. All that's going through my head right now isn't Lucas' child, but Paul's. What if it's Paul's child? Now it's not just the vodka making me dizzy. I can't do this. I need to get rid of this thing. Lucas knocks on the door.

"Hey, you've been in there a while. How's the test?"

"Ummmm…" Think, Laura. Think. "It's negative!" I yell through the door.

"No problem, honey! Better luck next time!" I hear him walk off to the bedroom. Shit, shit, shit, where do I hide this thing? I get up, wash my hands, and make my way to the kitchen where the trash can is. I dig to the bottom of the trash can and hide the test and its box under the rest of the garbage. I slip on my slippers, take the bag of garbage outside to the outdoor metal trash can, and scurry back inside. For now, I wash my hands, turn the TV off, put the vodka glass in the sink, all before heading to the bedroom. I tuck myself into the warm bed next to Lucas and spoon him from behind. I kiss his shoulder and tell him good night.

"Good night." he responds.

2:00am

"What the fuck is this?" Lucas questions.

"What?" I replied tiredly. I'm forced to wake up abruptly and my brain lags behind the aggressive tone of his voice.

"I found this outside." I open my eyes and look up at what he's holding. He's holding my pregnancy test. My heart drops and thuds in my stomach.

"How did you get that?" I ask.

"What do you mean 'get'? I woke up to the sound of a raccoon going through our garbage outside and found *your* pregnancy test on the ground in the pile while shoo-ing the bastard away."

"A fucking raccoon? That fucking bastard."

Lucas' face turns to a rare kind of anger I've only ever seen twice before. Only ever at his father at Christmas and at his drunk friend after he hurt a woman, but this glare and this deep primal voice has never pointed at me. His eyes are tearful with betrayal.

"Oh, so now I'm supposed to be mad at the raccoon for *your* lie? You're out of line, Laura! You're the one who's fucking lying! Why would you throw away your pregnancy test to hide it from me!?"

"Lucas, I'm sorry. I wish I could explain, but I'm scared. I'm sorry, honey!" I cry out

I can tell Lucas is trying to restrain his anger. As if he's mentally white knuckled, grasping the leash on the dog I had unleashed with my white lie. He's shuffling his feet as he hopelessly holds his bombardment of tears back. "I need to go." he concedes. He quickly leaves the room and I follow.

"Wait!" I beg.

"I don't want to yell at you, Laura! Leave me alone!" he continues to yell. He forces on his sneakers, just sitting half way onto his feet. He puts on a coat while still in his pajama bottoms. "I need to go somewhere. I need to drive. I can't handle this right now. I've been worried about your behavior, your drinking, your disrespect, and now I've boiled over. I need to drive somewhere because I still have the decency to not take my anger out on you!"

Before I can beg further, he's gone. The door is slammed, my adrenaline settles, and fear rises to the surface of my mixture of painful emotions. I don't know where he's going and I'm not going to try and chase him. Lucas barely had himself on together. Calling or texting him now would be explosive. He needs the space.

I start thinking about Paul. Oh, I fucking hate that bastard. This is all his fault. If he had never existed, this would've never happened. Lucas wouldn't be heartbroken and I wouldn't be pregnant with his… with this bastard of a fucking creature. The bruises are mostly gone, but I still feel their pain. My skin begs to leave my body when I think about how he came inside me. How he was able to get in my head somehow. Did he roofie me? Is that why I couldn't remember having sex with him? He said I had called him. Begged for him, even. Wait, no. I don't even have his number. I never go to Paul for anything, I always reach out to his dad if I need anything outside of work. He roofied me. He must have done *something* to me.

I walk back to the bedroom and grab my phone. I unlock it and go back to call history. There it is. I did call him. I even saved it, too. I stare at the number and it leers back at me. I move past the mental barrier of fear and confirm the phone call. I hold it up to my ear as it beeps. Time becomes slower and slower with every beep until I hear that outwardly friendly and familiar "Hello, Laura." I stare off into the organic swirls of the wood grain contained in the hardwood floor I stand on.

"Hey.", I said softly. "You were right. I need you right now."

I'm going to kill him…

I already feel as if I'm doing it as I'm driving down the unpopulated highway. I'm visualizing and feeling my arms exhausting themselves as I plunge my weight into the pocket knife through his chest. Warm blood splattering on my face, making it difficult to focus on how his body may defensively react to my attacks. The blood becomes tacky as each drip slows its pace as it crawls down my face. Fourth stab, fifth stab, sixth stab. My eyes are switching their attention from where my hands are, getting deeper into his chest with each thrust, and to his eyes, how his pupils roll back into his head as more of his blood creeps its way out his mouth, staining the crevices between his teeth and his gums. Tenth stab, sixteenth stab, twenty first stab. He tries to yell, but I'm pretty certain I've punctured his lungs far too many times for him to try to scream for help at this point.

I snap back to the present moment, breaking my fantasy. I'm still driving my car. My murder weapon of choice, a pocket knife previously mentioned, is tucked into the side of my black heeled boots, which reach about halfway up my knees. It's uncomfortable how it shifted around with each step I took from the front door to my car, as the boot's fit is somewhat loose around my leg, but it's the only good hiding spot for it in this sultry dress. I previously wore this deep scarlet satin dress on Lucas and I's wedding anniversary last year. It forms my body quite nicely, showcasing the best parts of my body. I don't know how I know where Paul lives. It's as if a part of me is guiding me there. It's an unconscious effort. Muscle memory, even. I take the next exit and make my way into a small suburban neighborhood, the roads illuminated by street lights. Right, left, left, right, left turns, until I reach his driveway. Paul's house isn't large by any means, it's only one floor, but it's all brick with a well kept front yard and an expensive looking stone footpath up to the door. It's surprising and a little funny to see his front yard better maintained than his hygiene or overall health for that matter. Props to whoever gets paid to deal with this weirdo's yard.

While reaching for the emergency brake to put the car into park, I finally realize just how soaked my hands are from sweat. Looking back at my steering wheel, I notice how my hands have left a wet impression of where they were previously. Even still, my hands are unconsciously looking for something to grip onto, which have now latched themselves to the seat belt currently hugging me. Am I nervous? I think I'm nervous. I've never killed anyone before, but I don't think I can continue living my life knowing this disgusting waste of a man takes up even the smallest amount of space on the surface of this Earth. I need him to occupy the space I know is reserved for him in Hell. Away from me, away from Lucas, and away from… our child.

Paul opens his door, his hallway light illuminating him from behind. Showcasing his silhouette. He gestures his hands for me to come inside. This is it. It's now or never, Laura. I release the latch of the seatbelt and exit my car. I'm not scared anymore.

"So then, I tell him, 'That's not how you twist it. This is how you twist it!'" he gestures his hands in the motion of masturbation, laughing loudly from his gut. I smirk, but quickly sink into my corner of the couch. My thumbs petting my glass of red wine. "Oh, come on, Laura. Isn't that funny?"

"Oh, yeah! It was!" I shoot up and force a slight giggle. Thank god he brushed his teeth before I arrived. All I have to do is get on top of him, kiss him, and while his guard is low, stab him. Stab him, stab him, stab him. Fuck, I haven't even made my move and I'm already feeling the adrenaline.

"You okay, Laura? Your eyes are glazed over a little bit there."

"Oh, um, yeah, I'm fine. I promise."

"Not still scared of me, are you? Because, y'know… I feel bad for what I did. I didn't mean to hurt you like that."

"Oh, no, I'm like, totally over it, you know?"

"You sure? You don't sound confident."

"Paul, it's water under the bridge." I stare at his eyes directly and confidently.

He smiles and continues. "Oh, good! I was really concerned you were still mad at me. Y'know, I've changed since all those months ago, right? I've had, let's say, a lot of time to reflect."

"Really? How so?"

"Oh, yeah. Tons of ways. For example, I've learned to listen more."

"Really. You?" I kid and force another giggle.

"Yeah, you wouldn't expect it, but I've become a great listener now. All I need is a little communication given to me."

"In what regard?"

He reaches for my breast and starts to caress it, leaning his face closer to mine. "Like, what can I do to make this feel better?" God, I want to vomit.

"I like how that feels currently" I respond. He grips a chunk of my hair and yanks my head towards him and our lips make an impact. Before I know it, his tongue has my mouth filled and grazes the back of my teeth with how deep he's trying to push it in. I'm bombarded with the dry taste of my red wine from my glass, his toothpaste, and the oak barrel essence from whatever brown liquor slivered from his glass moments prior. He takes his hand off my breast to grip my jaw and push my cheeks even closer to his face. His five o'clock shadow scrapes my face. Aggressive, sloppy, selfish. All the things I fucking hate about his man perfectly translates into the worst kiss of my entire life. A horrid collision of corrupt affection. I have to focus away from his misaligned attempt at pleasure towards moving my arms closer to him for an embrace, as much as I want to strangle what I'm almost reaching for, I'm feeling the same way as I did back in my office when he assaulted me. Instinctually, I'm frozen and I'm doing what I can to change my response from flight to fight. His hand begins to slide from my jaw down to my throat and he squeezes tightly before I can pull him in. This man has a vendetta against foreplay. I resist the hand he is using to grip my hair to release my mouth of the wet fleshy gag he has in my mouth to speak.

"Ahh, Paul, you're moving too quickly for me. Let's go slower." I'm trying to catch my breath.

He grips my hair even tighter and I wince in pain. "Nonsense. Communication is a two way street. You're gonna have to trust me like you did the first time we did this. You liked it then, you'll like it now."

"No, I'm trying to say I don't like it no-" he slaps me before I can finish my sentence.

"I love it when you act, bratty. Call me 'daddy'".

"No."

He pauses, loosens his grip, and stares at me. "You're gonna call me 'daddy'. Fucking do it."

I can't do this again. I can't do this. My instincts of safety and self preservation are lighting my senses on fire. Without hesitation or thought, I push him away, but the consequence is he grips my hair hard once again.

"I wanted to show you I've changed, Laura, but you're making me regret all the progress I worked so hard on making for myself."

I spit on him. "Fuck you." I exclaim.

In frustration, he punches me across my face and I fall off the couch. My head hits the coffee table and my glass of wine soon follows and spills beside my head. I can't tell if it's wine or blood soaking the carpet where my head rests. In my disorientation, I try what I can to track where his body is approaching me and I kick my feet in that direction. My first kick slips past his torso, my second lands in his leg, but my third, which would've hit him directly in his stomach is deflected by his arm and allows him to mount himself in between my legs. I'm trying futally to push him off, but he grips my hair again, pulling my hair as I push against him.

"You fucking slut!" he screams. "Why the fuck did you even come here if you don't even want to fuck!?" I keep kicking and pushing.

"Get the fuck off me, you creep!" I responded.

As if by a cruel, twisted, and sadistic chance of fate, in the flurry of kicks I attempted to get him off, the pocket knife I had stashed in my boot slipped out into the puddle of wine beside my head. We both freeze as we manage to figure out what each of us are thinking. He figured out I'm looking to spill blood, and now I know that he knows that.

"Laura." he pauses. "Is that your pocket knife?"

What the fuck do I say? No? Yes? I quickly try to grab the knife, but he strikes me again. One of my teeth in the corner of my cheek is out, but still hanging by its nerve. He grabs the knife, freeing my arm.

"Were you trying to kill me, Laura?"

I gather some macho to use my tongue to pluck my tooth from its attachment to my gum, as if pushing an apple off its branch. Blood quickly gushes from the hole it left. I spit my tooth at his face, my blood splattering him like a mosaic. As he winces, I reach for my empty glass of wine and slam it into his face, injuring my own hand in the process. He screams and leans back, dropping my knife beside me, which I quickly grab and open. Finally, I push my blade into his chest. It's easier than I imagined. The skin and bone makes little resistance against my knife. He falls on his back and I take my rightful position above him. Just like I had imagined before on the way over. The metallic taste of his blood found its way through my nostrils and the back of my tongue. My fingers slip and stick against each other as some are wetter than others. The drier ones are tacky from the blood's platelets sticking together. I just started stabbing him and I've already lost count so soon. I can't tell if he's failing at yelling or if I've just completely tuned it out. It's remarkable how resilient human beings are and how they've taken the reign of this planet as its conqueror, but still manages to be so fragile. Dying by a simple blade. The floor is pooled with blood and my knees slap against the soaked carpet with each thrust. He finally goes limp and his eyes have lost their light. I need to do more. I can't settle on just this. I marvel upon this work of art before I continue to rage. I sit on his legs, cut his shirt, and slice open his stomach. I reach in and pull out a menagerie of different colorful organs, but mostly intestines. I begin stuffing his open mouth with it.

"Fuck you!" I scream. "I'm in control now, you mother fucker! Eat this, you pig!" I don't care if he's not swallowing it, I'll stuff it all and force it down. As if I'm packing a sleeping bag, I inadvertently unhinge his jaw with my fists full of guts, but continue feeding him himself. I unzip his pants and pull them down and I move my panties to the side. I'm going to do this.

I'm in control now.

You want to know the most unforgivable part of all of this so far? The biggest twist of this entire story? How can Paul have *this* good of a shower and *still* look and smell like shit? There's three different steamy hot high-pressure streams of water exiting the shower heads from above, in front, and behind me. Luxury body wash included in this cacophony of scent, temperature, and sensation. Their scents, exquisite. The streams of water are hitting my naked body in his beautifully built shower in this gorgeous granite bathroom. A wonderful getaway spa located in this monster's dwelling. I needed to get his blood off somehow. After all, Paul certainly wasn't using it. I could melt into the drain along with his blood, this shower is so good.

Before I killed him, I really anticipated myself getting anxious and metaphorically shitting my pants about hiding his body and evading police, but honestly, I really don't give a shit at this moment. I feel like celebrating. Pop open another bottle of wine and marvel at the beautiful mess I made in the living room for a few hours, but I know that I should probably do something to hide my trail for when they eventually find his body. Not to mention, Lucas could be on his way home at this moment wondering where I am. That is, if he currently cares where I am.

I'm starting to wonder if I should've studied a bit more about hiding a body. Sure, I've watched my fair share of true crime documentaries at 11pm or occasional murder dramas, but in my circumstance, this is a big mess. Giant puddles of blood soaking and staining carpet, broken glass, signs of struggle, and I even spit on him— amongst other things. There's cuts and abrasions on my knuckles and fingers from force feeding him himself. Probably bits of my flesh in his mouth. I'm sure there's other pieces of evidence that I've left behind that I'm not even considering, but I think the biggest logical factors are hiding the body and murder weapon. I'm gonna say that the blood puddle in the living room is a lost cause. Whatever I'm gonna do, I'm gonna do it relatively quickly. Let's see.

I exit the shower and reach for a towel, but quickly realize that I probably shouldn't use it. Don't need to make more evidence by rubbing it all over my extremities. Guess the luxuries of tonight are over. I wring out what moisture is left in my hair into the shower drain and I put my dress back on while I'm still mostly wet. The fabric sticks to my skin as I put my boots back on.

I enter the living room and take another look at this mess. It's messier than I remember. I guess I played a little bit too much with his intestines. Of all the times to start feeling sick at this sight suddenly, it's now. His mangled flayed open corpse is for some reason finally making me nauseous, even after making him my play thing. His face is barely recognizable with how much I damaged his mouth from stuffing his organs into it. His neck looks even more inflated than usual and his lips are ripped from how stretched I had made them. I can't allow myself to puke here. I run back to the bathroom and bow myself over his toilet bowl and wretch until I puke the wine from earlier. Thankfully, it's all contained in the bowl. Cloudy red water with a coagulant of my stomach contents shifting in the body of liquid. I close the lid, and I flush.

As I'm washing my face in the sink to prepare the clean up in the other room, the mirror calls for my attention. Obedient to its call, I look up.

"Darling, oh, you poor poor thing. You just keep finding yourself in harsh situations, don't you?"

Bashful, I respond with "Yes, I suppose so".

"Look at yourself. You've made yourself sick. You're absolutely clueless and you're leaving such a mess and you plan to clean another. A delicate sweet creature like you should save your energy for more important matters." She softly caresses my cheek, subsiding the nervousness in my gut. "Like, Lucas.", she adds. My body relaxes and my shoulders go limp.

"Let me handle this clean up, Laura, dear."

She looks so beautiful and elegant. Like my mother. Her eyes carry kindness in her eyes. Her comfort is so delicious, I could sleep in her promise like a cradle.

"Your bloodlust might have faded, but mine hasn't. Let me do it, Laura. Let me handle this mess. Allow me to take care of you. Resssst, Laura… Rest."

In our hands, I close my eyes.

"Yes, please."

I feel myself crack a smile.

10:14am

The light above me flickers, breaking my spell. I blink and break my gaze at the door in the front of me. I look around and I'm in my office. To my left, the hole from before, the one I was knocked into, is bigger. It's about up to my shoulder height while I'm in my chair. The wires and pipes from behind the wall are more exposed than before. My bag, my coffee, my laptop, are all where I usually keep them. Surprisingly, even my beautiful missing red lunch bag. Neatly placed. A box of my things are packed and set directly in the middle of my desk. I'm dressed professionally. My button up shirt and fake dress pants. Hair tied up into a simple upstyle, not something I usually do.

I do not recall how I got here. My last memory is obvious. Paul's place. Oh, wait, Paul's place! His body! What the fuck happened? Did I hide the body? Where the fuck have I been? Where's Lucas? Is he still mad at me? Did I even go home? Obviously I did, I'm not dressed in my dress from that night and I got my things from home. What is going on?

Knock, knock, knock.

Oh my god, fuck! Breathe, Laura. Breathe.

"Come in!"

Either the door is slowly opening or I'm just perceiving it that way.

"Good morning, Laura."

It's Linkzy Sr.

"Oh! Ahem, ah, good morning, sir."

His face slightly tilts with curiosity as he notices my surprise.

"Are you, okay, Laura?"

"Yeah, yeah. Sorry. Your knocking just alarmed me. I'm kind of out of it this morning."

"Oh, I see… I'm sorry I startled you." He steps forward into my office and takes a seat in the chair in front of me, elbows resting on his knees. Seemingly unable to hold himself up somewhat.

"Um… Look, Laura. I don't know if you've heard today, but Paul's body was finally found."

"Oh— Oh my god. That's terrible!"

He takes a deep breath and his cigar scent hits my nose. There's a tinge of whiskey to it, reminiscent of his son.

"I appreciate the concern, Laura. I understand you and Paul were…" he sighs, scratches his head, and continues. "I understand the workplace relationship between you two was tenuous. I understand that and hold no judgment towards you. He certainly has his… idiosyncrasies."

"Yeah…" I replied. I think I officially hate that word now.

"At this point, with how… decayed his body was found… It'd be a miracle— I'm praying for a miracle from God for anything to be found, anything, to bring his murderer to justice."

I have nothing to say, but I continue to listen and stare at him. Patiently waiting for him to feed me more details.

"Are you sure he didn't call you or give you any indication on where he was going?"

"What do you mean?"

"You know. There was no warning or heads up for him to leave town. All they found at this house was a few indications that he may have skipped town. Drawers left open and clothes taken out. Toothbrush gone from the bathroom and suitcase indentation on his bed. That's all the details the police have given me."

"R-right. I'm... Glad you're finally telling me this" I replied. Another pause of silence stakes its claim in our conversation. He fights to speak more.

"I know you're leaving my company today, but just know you always have access to me and my contact information. Please... If you hear anything about Paul's murder or an email left unchecked... Again, don't hesitate to call me." His eyes begin to water. "I need to find whatever sick fuck did this to him."

I stare at him for a few moments as he hides his face into his hands before regaining his composure. His eyes are red and irritated from his body's attempt at crying, but he wipes away what he regrets showing me. He takes a large inhale and breathes out what stress his body allows him to release. Mentally, he's balancing on a skyscraper high tightrope; fighting high winds.

I then asked him "Did... did you say I'm leaving today?"

His eyes glare back up to mine, breaking his moment of turmoil in exchange for one of slight confusion. "Yeah? You gave me your letter four weeks ago... Your four week notice."

I take a moment to let this information marinade in my ears before it cooks into my brain.

"Mr. Linkzy, Sir... If you'll excuse me... I have to finish packing."

He stands up. "Of course. Be sure to let me know when you leave."

"Of course."

He leaves the room and the click of the door explodes. I stare down at my hands resting on my desk. Paul's teeth marks on my knuckles are just barely visible compared to the night I killed him. Four weeks?... Four fucking weeks? What— what happened? I get out my phone and check the date. Contained in my phone screen's glow screams today's date. A whole month. Gone. Seemingly, erased from my mind. I have to call Lucas. Where is he? I hurriedly clicked on my contact list and tapped his name, then the green phone shaped icon to call him.

Beeeep. Beeeep. Beeeep.

Click. "Hey, it's Lucas. Sorry I'm not available to take-"

I tap the red icon to hang up. I will make another attempt.

Tap.

Beeeep. Beeeep. Beeeep.

Click. "Hey, it's Lucas. Sorry I'm not available to take your call. Please leave a message after the tone and I'll try and call you back."

Tap, tap.

Okay. One more time.

Beeeep. Beeeep. Beeeep.

Click. "Hey, it's Lucas. Sorry I'm not available to take your call."

I let his message finish and ready myself to leave a message.

"Lucas, why aren't you picking up? I don't know what's going on. I can't remember the last four weeks. I'm scared and I don't know what to do. Please, call me back as soon as you can."

Tap, tap.

No point in trying to call again. I open my laptop and search for Paul Linkzy Jr. in an attempt to try and remember what happened to his body. It had made national news. All kinds of articles written by journalistic power houses to the smaller local outlets of news as well. Titles ranging from "Chitterling Killer " and "Man Splayed Open and Force Fed Himself". I clicked the first and most recent article mentioning his name, "Behind The Girl Who Found The Splayed Man".

"Four weeks ago, the son of an advertising entrepreneur Paul Linkzy Jr. went missing. Today, his body was found a remarkable two hundred and fifty miles away from his home in a suburb outside the city of Chicago, Illinois in a small forest on the property of a small family. Paul was found by the youngest daughter of said family, being 6 years of age. The corpse was severely damaged, with his internal organs stuffed into his mouth and throat, which wildlife later ate out of, including his mostly empty abdomen."

Oh, jesus. Poor girl.

12:46pm

Lucas still hasn't called me back. He's all I could think about as I packed. He's probably at work, sure, but I can't shake the uneasiness that I carry with the fact that I don't know what I've been doing these past few weeks. What have I said to him? Have I been treating him well? What have I been doing?

I'm walking down my work's hallways, passing the break room. Not a single person is in space. No Josephine, no Marcus, no Tom, no Other Marcus. None of my coworkers are present and it's dead quiet. No murmurs, laughs, or ringing phones. The lights are on the verge of giving me a headache, yet no hum. No ballet.

Senior's door is left open and I enter. He's sitting at his desk, leaning back drinking brown from a rocks glass.

"I'm heading out, Mr. Linkzy. I'll keep in contact."

Without breaking his stare at the ceiling, he reaches to shake my hand, which I oblige, and his arm relaxes back in his lap. Finally, his head turns forward to look at me.

"Best of luck to you, Laura. Thanks for sticking around."

"It was my pleasure."

I leave his office and as I walk towards my exit, I glance into the rooms, workspaces, and the familiar meeting room with the white board, this time blank and wiped clean. The skyline is as beautiful as ever and the sun shines onto the white cubicles, highlighting all the knick-knacks, notes, and small messes my coworkers adorned on their desks.

My final step into the elevator falls with increased gravity. Digging my foot into the well-worn carpet; the dirt of my decision, planted weeks prior. Grown into something beyond what I could've ever imagined. The doors close and they're more tarnished than before.

Down, down, down we go.

A pigeon slams itself into my windshield and I damn near drove myself off the fucking road. There's a grease spot left in the center of the glass. Wide and imposing. The rubber of my car's tires vibrates as I drive to, fro, and over the bumps designed to prevent sleeping at the wheel. I realign and focus my attention towards the painted lines. Once confident to be briefly blinded once more, I engage the cleaning fluid and wipers. The evidence of that surprise erased. All I can do is stay the course and pray that nothing makes my heart beat any faster than it already is.

Why hasn't Lucas gotten back to me? What did I do? I've called him so many more times within this car ride alone, I've begun to be afraid that I'm pushing him away more so than crying for his help. I would kill to be held in his arms right now. Safe, secure, and loved. A state of being where every single one of my problems fail at making logical connections to my state of worry and my fears fall away from the center of my mind, to the edges, and off into a cliff until they eventually make their return. A rest and an episode of true calm.

I've wondered if it's healthy to see my love viewed that way. Not a bonus to life, but a necessity. Something I live and breathe for. Where on my hierarchy of needs, Lucas is on the top of it. Wait, no, beyond the tip of the structure. Touching my stars and kissing the rings of my Saturn. I desperately need someone to tell me "as high as you want it, Laura. Put him as high as you need him to be." I'm begging to happenstance that when I walk through the door of our home, he'll be there. Arms open. Familiar, graceful, and welcoming.

I'm choosing not to imagine a home with the lights
turned off. His lack of presence. His missing warmth
would maintain a chill in the air that no blanket or blush
of red wine could replace. A memory liquor can never
make me shake off and forget. He is my husband. Truly,
the love of my life. I want to mix the jelly of our decay
and the eventual turning into our dust. I hope we will
always be intertwined and fated to fly in the wind
towards the oblivion above the tallest mountains. I need
a drink.

3:23pm

"Another." I proclaim, playfully.

He pauses and turns around to face me, or rather,
to face the back of my head. My forehead is resting on
my crossed arms on the sticky surface of the bar. There's
crumbs of bar snacks prickling the skin on my arms.

"Seriously?"

"Mmmmm-hm!"

"Look me in the eyes and say that, sweetheart."
He points his finger towards his eyes and smirks a sly
smile. I lift my head out of my arms and give the
bartender a drunken wink.

"Oookay" he says as he pours me another shot
of vodka. "But after this, I'm cutting you off." His eyes
glare back at me anticipating a response.

His arms look so lean, cut, and strong as he tilts
the bottle above the tiny glass. His shoulders are broad
and his chest is built into an enchanting V. The shirt he
wears fits him beautifully. A tasteful amount of stubble
on his face; an edgy look. A fresh haircut, and a large

chin is just the cherry on top of his handsome complexion.

"Noooo", I protest. "There's no need to do that. I'm feeling very fine and well minded." I dribble out.

His head shakes in an obvious show of disbelief, but he concedes to my request for more. More of the distraction I crave; the one that I desperately feel the need to drown myself into. When I drown myself enough, the noise of my anxious conscience is drowned out, too. My worries are as loud as artillery and my doubts pop like gunshots. Guilt has a sound that pelts you like a train horn. The demand for relief from this Hell screams in agony. Torture, even. Good luck trying to cover your ears. It's noise that resonates beyond your ears or conscience, but strums your nerve endings, plucks your ligaments, and carries its rhythm through your muscles and blood. It burns, contorts, bends, and breaks your spirit. Has its way with you. The only saving grace for me is the gentle quiet that liquor and sex draws from the shadows. Like you're in a crib again and you're stuck in the moment of your mother's lips gracing your forehead with a kiss. You float and sway in the cradle. You begin to be carried by the unknown. Concerns fade. You're whisked away into unremarkable and unmemorable moments. Finally, a long needed and anticipated dullness.

I'm going to try and sleep with this bartender. I'm well aware that he's simply taking advantage of me. I am always aware of men's intentions. Right from how they approach me with their greeting, I watch how they execute their plans every step of the way. I'm an anthrozoologist of sorts. Allowing this man to feed me vodka like saline in an IV, but I don't care and I don't want to care. I want to be able to confront his evil and live, but this is the only way I know how. The only way I can prove to myself that I have the capability to carry on from Paul, my high school ex, and all my other experiences of being robbed of my autonomy. Just let them have it. It's a demented cycle of losing control to feel in control. Pushing the rock up the mountain, only for it to fall.

Cheers to the void. My respite, my comfort. Mi Amore.

Chapter 9
Chomp, Gnaw, Chew

This pillow is twice as musty now as it was before. It's apparent it wasn't cleaned for a while before, but now its musk from the Bartender and the slightly oiled texture in the fabric of the pillow case makes it even more apparent now. How many nights of pomade and bar smoke live in this fabric? How many other women have stuffed their face into it like I had been? Held down by his brutal hand. His pomade and my breath are married in the seams now. Waiting for the next woman to join the harem of all of our scents and lack luster fucks.

The only tasteful thing about this pillow supporting my bad decisions are the goose feathers poking their way out of the pillow. Graceful, white, gentle, yet poking my crossed arms and my face. The pillow is soft, takes my shape, but lacks the fluff it had before my face went into it while he fucked me from behind. It's been flattened under our weight. You would've hoped he would have put as much effort into trying to make me cum as he does on achieving his conventionally shaped biceps, but as expected, he is a selfish lover. "Lover" being a generous word. An orgasm was hoped for, but the lack thereof was an inevitability that I had always known to be the truth. However, the sense of control I was looking for was all that I needed. I've sobered up, but still wide awake. He's assumedly comatose from his orgasm. I'm more than satisfied, but still can't find it in myself to sleep. Lucas is on my mind.

My soul would curl if I didn't have him, but I don't deserve him.

I can toss and turn until my mind truly exhausts itself? Maybe I can masturbate? Am I even in the mood right now? My phone is out of battery, so no social media. No. No, I'm going to go home. My own bed. Lucas and I's scents. My own marriage, but also to charge my phone. Maybe he's called. Fuck, I miss him so much.

Quietly, I turn my legs towards the edge of his bed and plant my feet down onto his dirty laundry on the floor. In the dark, I search for my dirty laundry. He had taken them off me and thrown them around his room like party streamers or a child ripping wrapping paper off of his gifts for his birthday. Stupid with glee. Vicious and feeding off of an adrenaline rush. Rabid like an animal. A brand new play thing. Something he'll lose interest in after his fantasies and imagination have come to fruition. My bra, panties, my pants over there. Oh, my earring hiding in the folds of my shirt. It falls to the carpet as I lift it up. I didn't notice that my earring came off. It was a gift from Lucas. Glad I'm not leaving it here.

His body shifts and he turns as my belt buckle jingles as the leather strap slivers around my waist. I grasp the metal with my palm to mute the sound, but I was too careless and it's too late.

"Hey, where are you going?" he mumbles through his pillow.

Fuck. No need to sugar coat my response.

"I'm going home." I monotone

He pulls his covers over himself a little more and exhales.

"Hmmm. Okay. See ya.", he responds.

Huh. I was expecting him to at least give a feign courtesy of care to offer to sleep over for the night, but whatever. I finish dressing myself, grab my bag, and leave.

Section 31

It feels like it's been an eternity since I've seen the front of the door of our home. I'm sad at just how comforting it looks. Arms reaching out for a hug; weary. An embrace from a whole other life that I feared had faded away. I'm scared. I take a deep breath, and finally push through the fear to see what I've been avoiding. I put my key into the door knob, turn it, and activate the knob to step forward into my home.

A wind of high pressure releases from the widening crack of the doorway and a putrid smell emerges. The blinds are closed and the lights are off. It's almost pitch black as my hand reaches for the light switch. I can't see much beyond the hall leading to the living room. Grazing and searching for the switch to flick. My attention was drawn forward at the discovery of this crypt. My finger discovers it and the light is just strong enough to reveal the mess. Garbage everywhere. Pizza boxes, wrappers, new papers, junk mail, condoms, receipts, moldy food, sticky dried spilt coffee on the hardwood floors. The carpets are ruined by dark dried puddles, muddy footprints, and the couch is in shambles. One of the legs is broken and leaning off to the side. It's fabric torn, shredded, and molested. Cigarette butts are decorative accents to the piles of trash festering throughout the apartment. The kitchen is unrecognizable. Seemingly, the sink has disappeared into the visual noise of filth. There's beer cans, glasses, dirty plates, and a mirror for coke on the kitchen island. Scratched and absent of its reflection. Well worn in pursuit of hapless bits of scrape.

I wretch over to gag. Hoping to puke, as the taste and smell of last night's vodka would taste better than the foul humid air. It's searing acidity would be a better hug. A deranged menagerie of mire lies throughout my home. Splatters, fuzzes, and shadows moving with each step I take forward. I'm helplessly holding my shirt over my nose and mouth in a sad attempt to save my senses from this Hell.

All I can do is crumble. Fall to the floor on my hands and knees. Tuck myself into my body and pretend to be a fetus. Sheltering myself from this nightmare. My form becomes one with the piles of rot and plastic. I allow myself to become one of them. Lucas isn't home. The garbage is the family I've inadvertently been working towards. The embrace that I felt at the door, reaching for me, wasn't of the old solace, but of my purgatory. I am damned to weep.

Section 32

Buzz.
Buzz.
Buzz…

Buzz.
Buzz.
Buzz…

I reach for my phone. It's been sticky from sitting in… something. The stain on the bed sheet has been staring at me ever since I collapsed beside it hours prior. It smells unrecognizable and its appearance is rustic.

Buzz.

Buzz

Bu- click…

"…"

"…"

The silence is broken by a "Hello?" on the other end.

"Lucas?", I inquired.

"No. My name is Detective Gongsun. Is this Laura Alders?"

"…" I'm too tired to speak. I haven't drank water since God knows when and it's hoarse from inactivity.

"Hello? Laura?"

"Sure… This is her."

"Oh, hi, there Mrs. Aalders. I apologize for disturbing you. I'm currently working the case for the murder of your former boss, Paul Linkzy. Do you have a moment to talk?"

"…"

"Hello?"

"Yes, I'm here." I assure them. "Yes, I have a moment to talk."

"Wonderful. I have just a few questions I need to run over with you."

"Uh huh." I mutter blankly into the dark.

"Where were you the night of April 29th?"

"Oh…" I allow myself to wonder. "My husband and I had a really bad argument at home"

"Okay. So, you were at home the whole night?"

"No, I wasn't. I had left."

"Left to go where?"

I pause before continuing.

"Left to go blow off some steam."

"Like, did you leave to go to a twenty four hour gym? A bar? Where did you go?"

"I went to Paul's house."

"…"

"…"

"You… Went to Paul's house?"

"Yes, detective."

"What did you two do? Did he say he was going somewhere? Meeting someone?"

"No, he didn't."

"Okay. Why didn't you come forward with this information sooner? He's been missing for a number of weeks."

"…"

"…"

"I was afraid."

"…"

"…"

"That's understandable, but you should've come forward sooner."

"I'm aware. I'm not afraid any more."

"…"

"…"

"So, what did you and Paul do?"

"We just talked.

"Talked?"

"Talked."

"You talked about what, Laura?"

"Oh… Things."

"What kind of things?"

"Topics." I mutter.

"Laura, stop playing games with me. What did you and Paul talk about?"

"Stuff."

"Laura, this isn't a joke."

"Isn't it?"

Knock, knock, knock.

My attention bolts up from the bed. Did I hear that correctly? Am I hallucinating?

Knock, knock, knock.

"Hello? Laura? Are you there?" Was that the phone or the door? My heartbeat accelerates and I'm panicked. I gain control of my numbed legs and carry myself out the room and towards the front door, leaving my phone on the bed. Rushing forward.

Knock, knock, knock.

I open the door and the sun beams down on me, and my eyes squint to adjust to the light.

"Laura. Oh my god."

It's Lucas. My beautiful goofy Lucas. My arms rush towards him and I hold on for dear life, as if I'm about to fall.

"Lucas! Oh my god. Oh, Lucas." I weep. I stumble down his jacket and further down to where I'm embracing his legs. His knees become wet from my tears.

"Laura, oh my god. You look sick." he peers into the apartment. "Oh my Christ, what happened to the apartment? What the fuck happened?"

"Hell, Lucas! Hell happened! I didn't know where you went! I didn't know what happened! I don't remember anything! I've been falling apart without you!" I get back up and start kissing his cheek. He pulls away.

"Laura, you smell like shit. It looks like you haven't showered in days."

"Please, come inside. I need you inside. I need to talk to you." I pull him past the threshold on the front door and he begins to gag at the smell of the mess. He tries to protest, but he can't speak past his body's instinct. The door closes behind him once he's inside and I turn the light on.

"Oh, Jesus fucking Christ, Laura." he decries.

"Where were you? Why were you avoiding my calls?" I question as I drag him into the living room.

"Laura, I was avoiding you."

I stop in my tracks. "You were… what?"

"Laura, I've been trying to avoid you. I've been with my mother. She had gotten so many calls from you that we almost considered filing a restraining order." he's covering his nose and mouth with his jacket.

"She lied to me?"

"Laura, do you not remember how you were treating me? The screaming, the throwing objects, the arguments?"

"No, Lucas! I don't! I'm sorry I don't remember from after Paul died. That's why I've been calling you."

His train of thought pauses. He exchanges a perplexed concerned stare with his eyes and treads carefully into his next muffled words.

"What does this have to do with Paul?"

There's that veil of silence once more. Another secret in the form of a whisper, however this time, hesitant and scared.

"I killed him…" I utter.

His head slightly turns and leans forward. Brows furrowed. "You… did what?"

"I killed him, Lucas." I repeated. I'm praying he heard me that time. This confession burns my lips to reveal.

"I… I don't understand" he responds. "That's… You're not… like that…" His eyes glaze and look past me. Trying to comprehend and digest this truth. "There's no way-"

"Lucas! I killed him, Lucas! I killed him!" I interrupt.

The protection of his jacket falls from his face. He's scared. "I don't understand. There's no way… There's no way!"

"I went over there and I stabbed him! I stabbed him probably a hundred times! Tore him open and-"

"Laura! You did what was in those articles? Tore his guts out and force fed him his-?..." Finally, all the tension and nervousness his face had been expressing has spread to his stomach. He vomits.

"Lucas, I did what was best for us! He just kept **fucking** pestering me. That fucking disgusting, vile, wretched excuse for a human being. He made me feel like I was burning from the inside. I felt so helpless and scared. I couldn't go on living my life feeling knotted up and twisted inside! I wouldn't be able to look into my child's eyes without feeling that fear of him out there, Lucas! I couldn't have that disgusting fucking rapist animal walking the streets with our children around! I love you! I love you so fucking much! I love our child! You're the love of my life! I needed him dead!" Lucas slaps me across my face. I'm stunned. He's frozen and looks as if he's seen an incomprehensible fear. White, flushed, and sorrowful. Terrified.

"You… You had every right to feel scared, Laura. I was scared, too. Scared for you." he utters. "But… You hurt me, Laura." His face scrunches into remorse. His face red with devastating sadness. "You hurt me really really badly… You scared me. You made me lose faith in you, Laura… I can't trust you to not hurt me anymore… I can never do those things with you, Laura. Not after… this… Laura, I can't… Laura… Wha-… What have you done?"

I can't help but to start to hyperventilate. My hands are wet from sweat and my nightmare comes alive. My body has the instinct to wail and panic. *Run away! Run away! Wait, no, hug him. Wait, no, you'll scare him. Save this. Don't let it end.* My thoughts scream. This simply can't be it. This can't be over. Can it?

"Wha-what do you mean, Lucas? I had to do it! I fucking had to! He was in my head and I couldn't stop thinking about his blood!"

"Laura, please! You're scaring me!"

"You fucking liar! You never fucking loved me!"

"I don't want to have another argument, Laura! Just take this!" he reaches into his inner jacket pocket, takes a folded packet out, and hands it to me. I look at its rectangular white shape and take it out of his hands. I open it up.

"It just needs your signature, Laura. Please… Please sign it so I can leave. I- I can't keep looking at

you like this. You need help. You are severely ill. I don't
even know who you are any-" I leap at him before he
can finish his sentence. His body crashes to the floor and
his head follows it with a crack.

"You're never going to leave me, Lucas! I love
you, Lucas!"

"Laura! No, please! Get off of me! Let me
leave!"

"No! I've done too much for you, Lucas! You
wouldn't fucking be here if I hadn't saved you from your
father! You lived with the Devil! You'd still be his little
fucking sex toy if it wasn't for me! He would've raped
you all throughout college if I hadn't given you a place
to live! I fucking saved you! You owe me!"

"I don't owe you a fucking thing, Laura! Let me
fucking leave!"

"Never!" I boom. I reach for a glass bottle,
break it against the wall, and plunge it into his neck. His
eyes widen and his warm blood spurts onto my face and
arms, dripping back down to his open, shocked, mouth.
He gargles his own blood harshly and flails his arms,
slapping and slipping against my wet red head. I keep
throwing my arms into his direction. Haphazardly
slashing and puncturing him. His attempts at flailing
become weaker and shaky. His skin goes paler, his eyes
roll back. I slow my flurry of attacks. The solid squirts of
blood slip into weak sputters. He's covered in wounds,
gashes, slices, and scrapes. It's hard to tell exactly where
his stream of blood is pushing itself out from, but now
it's down to a simple gush all over, then just streams of
drips. I look down below me. My dead husband. The

man I worshiped and aspired to be like. I don't want him to leave.

I take the dirty bottle and scrape it against his chest with all my weight, the bottle shattering bit by bit with each pull. Peeling his skin and muscle off bare until the white of his ribcage is revealed to me. I use all of my might to separate the protective cage surrounding his lungs and reach for his heart just beyond the space between them. I pull it towards my face. The tissue attached to it stretches and does what it can to stay in its place, but it's useless. His heart is mine and I take my first bite. I savor his saltiness before I go in for the second. For the third, my face is deep enough into the muscle for it to paint my whole face rusty. It takes a lot to break a piece from itself. It's almost rubbery and it takes a bit to chew. The front door is kicked down. It's might shook the pictures of Lucas and I's wedding off the wall. Shattering upon impact with the floor.

"Freeze! Hold it right, there! Laura Aalders, you're under- oh, Christ…"

A whole squadron of uniformed men stand in place as my face turns towards the light from behind them and the lights in their hands.

Their light illuminates my tears. Faithful, even in hardship.

The End.